Instructions for the Drowning

INSTRUCTIONS *for*

the DROWNING

Stories

Steven Heighton

A John Metcalf Book

Biblioasis
Windsor, Ontario

FIRST EDITION

10 9 8 7 6 5 4 3 2 1

Library and Archives Canada Cataloguing in Publication
Title: Instructions for the drowning / Steven Heighton.
Names: Heighton, Steven, 1961–2022, author.
Description: Short stories.
Identifiers: Canadiana (print) 20220259917 | Canadiana (ebook) 2022025995X |
ISBN 9781771965354 (softcover) | ISBN 9781771965361 (ebook)
Classification: LCC PS8565.E451 I57 2022 | DDC C813/.54—dc23

Edited by John Metcalf and Ginger Pharand
Copyedited by John Sweet
Cover and text designed by Ingrid Paulson

Grateful acknowledgement to the publications in which some of these stories appeared in earlier form: *Ambit, Event, The Fiddlehead, Globe and Mail, Granta, Threepenny Review, The New Quarterly, New England Review, PRISM International,* and *Zoetrope: All-Story.* "The Stages of J. Gordon Whitehead" was first published as a chapbook by Frog Hollow Press.

Published with the generous assistance of the Canada Council for the Arts, which last year invested $153 million to bring the arts to Canadians throughout the country, and the financial support of the Government of Canada. Biblioasis also acknowledges the support of the Ontario Arts Council (OAC), an agency of the Government of Ontario, which last year funded 1,709 individual artists and 1,078 organizations in 204 communities across Ontario, for a total of $52.1 million, and the contribution of the Government of Ontario through the Ontario Book Publishing Tax Credit and Ontario Creates.

PRINTED AND BOUND IN CANADA

Contents

Instructions for the Drowning
1

Repeat to Failure
13

As If in Prayer
33

Expecting
45

Professions of Love
71

You're Going to Live
91

Who Now Lies Sleeping
99

Everything Turns Away
125

Desire Lines
145

Notes Toward a New Theory of Tears
161

The Stages of J. Gordon Whitehead
179

Instructions
for the
Drowning

Ray's father once told him that if you ever jumped into the water to help a drowning man, he would try to pull you down with him and there was only one way to save yourself and him as well. Drowning men were men possessed and they were supernaturally strong. But they were also as weak as babies, seeing as they had lost all self-control.

His father shook his head, his lips clamped thin, as if such a loss were the most pitiful any man might suffer. You could neither wrestle nor reason with a man in that condition, he explained. In a sense, he was hardly human anymore.

Ray—ten or eleven years old—had pictured the victim metamorphosing into a kind of ghoul, sinewy and slippery as the Gollum he had been imagining while reading *The Lord of the Rings.*

So you would have no choice, his father concluded, his eyes narrowing and hardening behind the steel-rimmed spectacles, a gaze that always preceded a briefing on some unfortunate but unavoidable masculine duty. A drowning man would have to be knocked out cold. For his own good. A short, clean punch to the side of the jaw—that would be the preferred blow. After which you could easily complete the rescue, towing the victim in to shore. (In the boy's adaptation, the victim was tamed from raving fiend to serenely compliant human, slightly smiling, eyes closed, like those cartoon characters who always looked so gratified to have been knocked out.)

How rescuers who were not world-class water polo players were to find the leverage and stability to land a decisive blow while being dragged underwater by a panicking man was not a question the boy could have formed or would have posed. If his father said the operation worked—and he made it sound like one performed routinely in the summer lakes of Canada and the northern states—then it must.

Over the years Ray would hear other men, usually older, mention the technique often enough to gather that it had once been endorsed, if not actually practised, by a whole generation. Now it seems as dubious and dated as the quaint medical certainties of another age. Yet this afternoon, as Ray's wife, Inge, floating near the end of the dock, cries out and begins splashing and coughing, it's not the sensible modern rules of aquatic rescue that first leap to mind but his old man's advice. Then comes the thought that he's not even sure what the modern rules are. He springs up out of the fold-out recliner and pulls off his sunglasses, his latest can of IPA tipping and rolling off the dock. The blood drains from his head—he is almost drunk, he was almost asleep—and the glasses slip from his hand as he stands swaying. His sight returns. There's Inge, treading water effortlessly, using just one arm. Her sunlit face is strained. Another cough hacks out of her, but then she calls hoarsely, "It's OK—OK!"

"What? You sure?"

"Just a cramp. My leg. But I think it's . . ."

. "Inge?"

She winces, her teeth white in the sun. From the other direction, behind Ray, a jocular voice calls down, "Hey, you two lovebirds all right down there?"

"OK!" he shouts back automatically toward the cottage, where their hosts, Hugh and Alison, have retired for a little nap, as Hugh always puts it. Hugh and Alie enjoy a spirited, irreverent rapport, playfully and publicly physical. In the penumbra around them, other couples in their circle are never quite free of a sense of deficiency and demotion.

With a choked groan Inge vanishes as if something has yanked her feet from below. She flails back up, arms flapping and reaching. She could be a woman playing the victim during a lifeguard training session or someone just gauchely fooling around. No. She is a decent swimmer and she is no joker; she laughs readily enough with her friends and with Ray, even these days, but she dislikes physical comedy and April Fool's pranks of the kind that Hugh loves to devise.

Ray charges down the dock and jumps off the end where a half-empty wineglass perches as if on the edge of a bar. The water here is deep, but he dives flatly, smacking his paunch and his groin and surfacing fast. He is an ugly swimmer, a heaver and splasher, his head always turtled above the water—he hates submerging his face—but he is strong, and padded enough that he floats.

All that's visible of Inge is her face tipped sunward like a tiny, shrinking island. He calls, "Hang on!" and she stammers back, "Help, help, help me now, Ray!" It's a shock to hear *help* used right on cue and exactly as it should be. And her accent—for as long as they have known each other it has been faint, but for rare spasms of anger or passion. Now it's thickly Dutch. Her face dips under, comes back up, her mouth gawping, hands flogging the water. "I'm here," he says, and extends his left hand. "Inge?" She launches toward him. Her facial muscles flex and contort and he gets a flashback of that gurning creature conjured up by his father's words some thirty years ago. Her eyes—pure blue, no pupil—do seem half-alien, perceiving but not knowing him.

She hugs and envelops him, the way she might an exciting new man, as perhaps she already has, who can say? They've been sleeping separately for almost a year, although not on this visit, and the bed sharing up here is not merely for show or to pre-empt gossip—and Hugh and Alie are gossips—no, they really are trying to give it one more shot, and the sex last night was good, partly because it had been a while and partly because of the fresh setting and the voluptuous breezes floating in, and also, sure, because they both knew without saying a word that they would team up and show Hugh and Alie, ostentatiously coupling in the next room, that they too had a marriage.

Her skin last night was hot as always, much hotter than his. Her crushing embrace now is icy. She's all over him, clinging to him like the one thing afloat on an empty sea. *Grasping at straws*. Now he gets it. It's not about drawing lots but about grabbing handfuls of the useless stuff floating up from the hold of a sinking ship.

She's pulling him down. Grappling—*Inge, don't!*—an arm, trying to wrench free. Impossible, just like his father said. His eyes are above the water, then below: a glimpse of locked, thrashing forms, bubbles swarming, her skinny white legs hooked around his waist.

They surface. He inhales a breath, she choking and gasping. Somehow he's facing the shore. Hugh and Alie, in the matching aqua sarongs from their March holiday in Goa, are running down the flagstone steps from the cottage. Inge is climbing Ray as if he's a dockside ladder—his knees, his thighs, his shoulders the rungs. Kicking her way up, she forces him down. Water floods his yelling mouth and he gags, digs her clawing grip off his shoulder, fends her off with both hands, flattening her breasts under the one-piece she always wears up here because of Alie, who makes her untypically shy. *Nice*, she says, *I get the pot-belly but not the baby*, though it's not really much of a belly, not compared with his. She surges toward him again. He parries her arms, but her legs pincer around his hips with fantastic strength and she pulls him back down. *You're going to kill us both! Inge!* Her face underwater is deathly pale and yet frantically alive, wild eyes unseeing, hair billowing. He grabs at the surface, the light, somehow drags them both back up. He spews out water and gasps. Without thinking or revisiting his father's crazy advice, he hits her.

7

The blow misses the jaw—*the jaw,* as if it's any old jaw, not Inge's jaw—and grazes her cheek. Her eyes open even wider. He has never hit her—though a few times recently her charged silence made him wonder if he would have to duck a punch of hers. He has never punched anyone, not since grade school. He forgets whatever technical instruction his father once gave him. Her legs pincer tighter. Feet scrabbling for traction, he swings again. At the same time, she jerks her head sideways, toward the blow, reinforcing it. Fist and jaw meet with a crack and her eyes roll upward. Her leg-grip slackens, her whole body sags. Panting, spitting, he half turns and cradles her torso with his left arm, scooping at the water with his right. "It's OK. I'll get us back. I'm sorry. Hang on." He frog-kicks, hindered by her dragging legs, aiming for the dock where Hugh and Alie now loom, leaning forward, hollering like swim coaches exhorting their athletes on the home stretch.

Inge tenses, twitches as if snapping out of a doze. He looks at her face on his shoulder. Her reopened eyes focus. Her fist leaps out of the water like a fish and she clouts him square in the nose, slipping under after she connects. "Jesus, Inge!" His eyes, already blurred, tear up from the punch. He twists free of her. Hugh and Alie stand staring, hands lax at their sides, as if it's occurring to them that maybe no one is drowning here, maybe Ray and Inge are just having a fight—a real, physical fight, not like a professional couple on a long-weekend getaway but like a pair of locals, those trailer park townies whose bonfire parties at the public beach down the shore so obviously test Hugh and Alie's liberal tolerance . . . All of this he absorbs in a moment as he opens his mouth to call out—but then Inge jumps him from behind and hauls him back under. He tears at the pale, magnified hands clamping his rib cage, the rigid fingers with their bitten nails. Around them the water grows darker, colder. Bubbles boil upward in silence, lighting a route back to the surface. Suddenly, already, it looks too far. He could surrender, he could just inhale, it would be less painful, painless, he has heard, but he rips himself free as if from a jammed seat belt in a sinking car and shoots upward.

Sunlight detonates. His lungs erupt, shooting out water, blood as well, his nostrils hot with blood, his eyes half-blind. She pops up beside him, gagging and coughing. She throws another, limper punch but misses. He is breathing ammonia, briny mucus. She rears toward him again as if to attack, but no, she is churning, sputtering past him on the right, toward the dock, seemingly restored by her rage. He's furious himself now. Alie is calling in a thick and breaking voice, "It's all right, you two. Don't worry. Come on. Just come in!"

Ray keeps coughing, though weakly. He's still in trouble, in fact, and could probably do with a little help himself. Hugh is tearing off his sarong, crouching, flicking it out so that one end trails in the water like a rope, a few strokes short of Inge's reach as she labours toward the dock. Hugh should be naked now but isn't. (Is that underwear?) Beside his splayed feet, Inge's wineglass still stands. Alie is poised to dive in, but Hugh cups a hand over her kneecap; Inge is managing just enough not to need rescuing. "It's OK, girl!" Alie says, kneeling down beside Hugh, her voice throbbing. "You're there!"

Ray's legs feel heavy as anchors and his pummelling heart skips beats as he side-strokes toward the dock, toward Inge, who now grabs the floating end of the sarong with both hands. Hugh stands up—he actually is wearing underwear, baggy white boxers—and tows her in. She glances back at Ray. Her stricken gaze might be fixed on a dangerous pursuer or, yearningly, a loved one falling behind in the course of some desperate escape. One of her hands releases the taut sarong as if she means to point, wave, beckon. Alie grabs the free hand and tugs upward; Hugh reaches down as well; Inge is suspended off the end of the dock, continuing to gaze back at him.

It occurred to him later that the crisis, from the moment he realized she was in trouble until he himself was dragged up onto the dock, could not have taken more than three minutes. A few hundred heartbeats. It felt interminable, of course. His memories—resolving into vivid fragments, like violent few-second cellphone videos posted on a news site—felt hyper-real and indelibly stable, as if exempt from memory's normal fading and smudging.

But he could not test their accuracy by discussing them with Inge. Her refusal to revisit the crisis—their near deaths, their mutual violence, her once-in-a-lifetime relinquishing of all self-control—was hardly surprising, especially given what they learned soon afterward. Still, in spite of everything, she surprised him the following year by wanting to return to the lake for their customary long-weekend stay. Hugh, he warned her, would certainly try to discuss the incident and his and Alie's own roles in it. But Inge was adamant. She seemed to view the return not so much as a form of trauma exorcism but rather as a way of salvaging an important tradition, in a matured, familial form. She meant to swim as much as ever (though in the end, as it turned out, she chose not to go back in at all). As for Hugh and Alie, she realized they could be annoyingly self-satisfied, but they were true friends and that mattered more than ever now.

For the first five years of their marriage, Inge and Ray had tried to have a baby, suffered miscarriages, consulted specialists, and in due course accepted that there would be no children. No way to know if children would have prevented or accelerated the fraying of their marriage over the following three years, leading up to that struggle in the lake. But a few weeks after it, trying to work out the details of a separation, they discovered Inge was pregnant. At first, pending the re-test, she was tense, touchy, guarded, as if she dreaded either outcome; with the second positive, an unqualified joy overcame her, an *exultancy* that seemed to astonish her as much as her condition. Ray, his two black eyes now faded to yellow, felt himself bumped into the role of designated worrier, the sober, tentative one, although he too felt more pleased by the surprise than he would have predicted. That the summer's lone interlude of carnality, however mutually satisfying, had resulted in conception—a result supposedly impossible—made him wonder, ever so slightly, if Hugh could have been responsible.

The boy was born in April. He could not have looked more like Ray. At the cottage in August, their first afternoon, after Hugh and Alie had retired for their nap, Inge, on the dock, unwrapped Isaac and handed him down to Ray, who was standing in the shallows by the tiny beach.

"Inge, are you sure?"

"Don't be silly, Ray. Go on, let him get the feel of it."

Ray held his naked son so that the boy faced away from him, out over the lake, Ray's hands all but encircling the rib cage and feeling the thudding of the tiny heart. He dunked him to his navel. Isaac's pale legs began frogging promisingly, his whole body writhing as if longing to be released.

Repeat
to
Failure

September is the Monday of months, the world lurching back into gear; a month of heavy lifting by bodies and minds summer-spoiled and rusty. But this year Rasmus felt equal to the change. It didn't seem the latest annual prompt or memorandum about accruing debts and limitations, that sense of dragging ever farther behind. He had forgotten how love can lighten the body and pause time.

Still, that very morning he'd been reflecting on freakish ways to die. A social media friend he'd never met had posted news about a mutual contact, likewise unmet, who'd been killed after part of the landing gear of a commuter aircraft had detached on the plane's approach to the airport of a city out west. The victim, whose name Rasmus could not remember, was playing a round of golf at an empty course—it was a drizzly Monday morning— beside the airport. The debris hadn't hit and killed him directly but instead startled him as he steered a golf cart up a fairway. Reportedly the object plunged earthward with a screeching whistle and just after it struck the ground, embedding itself deeply—or so Rasmus pictured—the driver veered the cart and one wheel had slid over the steep, wet edge of a sand trap. The cart toppled and rolled. It was a deluxe cart with a second, rear-facing bench; the two back passengers spilled clear and were unharmed, if shaken up. The front bench rider, though bruised and mildly concussed, was able to walk away.

But the cart crash hadn't killed the victim any more than the object had. As luck would have it, he'd been snacking while he drove, some kind of energy bar. It wasn't clear whether, having swerved to avoid the falling debris, he'd choked on a mouthful in the chaos of the crash, or whether he'd gasped in fear and aspirated what he was chewing.

In the confusion, his friends failed to realize what was actually wrong until too late. Maybe they pulled him clear of the upended cart and one man knelt and performed chest compressions. A second—Rasmus imagining now—sat on the edge of the sand trap, one hand to his bleeding head, one hand holding a phone to his lips. Maybe the third man in a daze had slowly approached the half-buried piece of steel, crouched down as if lining up a putt, gingerly felt the steel. (*Would* it have been hot? Objects falling through the upper atmosphere heated up, even ignited, but they were flying at meteoric speed.)

On his way to the gym at lunch, Rasmus pondered the long-shot intersection of the variables. As improbable as dialing the tumblers of a Swiss bank safe into alignment by chance. Or call it *malignment:* a piece of the plane breaking free at that particular moment, say one in ten million; falling directly in front of the one cart on a vacant fairway on a deserted golf course, one in two million; the cart happening to be skirting, too closely, a deep sand trap on wet grass, maybe one in five thousand; one of the four men at that moment snacking, that man happening to be the driver, etcetera etcetera. Multiply the factors. Stupefying odds.

Every lunch hour for a few months now he'd walked from the office, where he worked for a medical equipment firm as a supply chain manager, to the gym. They say a man puts on weight when he's ready to settle down—or is it when he meets the right woman? Rasmus had emerged from a lawyer-ridden divorce and met that woman—not younger, as with his separated or divorced peers, but three years older. She was a psychotherapist who worked with preteen and teenaged girls and who, with disarming openness, acknowledged that losing her parents in adolescence had steered her away from parenthood and toward her clientele.

Older or not, she was fitter than Rasmus and also, he felt, sharper, more vital, in fact incandescent with health, intelligence and—despite social changes that had made her field busier and more dispiriting by the year—optimism. In the pulsing glare of that positivity Rasmus felt dull, doughy, blunted and tarnished by the past decade of dissatisfactions, early mid-life.

He could have opted simply to believe her when she told him she loved him as he was and he was wrong about himself—that all she wished he would do differently is join her at yoga once or twice a week, to loosen him up physically and psychically. Tia was not one for lies, tactful or otherwise. Yet in this one case he irrationally chose to believe she must be lying. Hence his current broad-spectrum campaign of self-improvement. He was reading books as he once had, mainly non-fiction; he was rationing time online; he was shunning unhealthy food (his mother was a nutritionist— he knew how to do it); he was working out.

Most days, Rasmus shared the change room with other middle-aged male professionals whose chests and groins— shaven, while their thighs and bellies remained centaurishly hirsute—flagged them as now in a relationship with a young woman. The gym was a recently opened, three-floor facility as cool, immaculate and echoing as a new international departures concourse. The filtered air flowing discreetly from the many grilled ducts was clean as freezered vodka and odourless as vapour from the stratosphere. Once, arriving at noon on the dot, he heard the gym's playlist of bleating auto-tuned pop being tweaked down until it was barely audible. Another time, as he left a bit late, right at one (he'd been waiting for Tia to emerge from her low-lights yoga session) it flared back up to its pre-noon volume. "I guess old man hour is over," he'd told Tia, whose skin looked dewy, preternaturally renewed by her hour in the dim yoga room, the whites of her eyes clear as a child's.

"Old man, right. As if you need to punch in here every day. But I want you to try this Quantum Flow class. Goofy name, but it's amazing."

It was the one thing she did at the gym, a weekly hour that ended with a ten-minute *shivasana*—corpse pose—during which most of the participants would drift off, she said, including her. The teacher, a young cellist with a full brown beard and the immense green eyes of a Miyazaki figure, favoured Renaissance lute music at low volume. It was the one place in the gym you could escape the playlist with its racing, algorithmically unified tempo. "This downtown," Tia had said, "is still *accelerating* at noon and it keeps going till everything falls apart at five. Thousands of drivers wired like long-distance truckers who haven't slept in days. Day after day, repeat till failure. That yoga room . . . it's like the one corner of your mind that stays calm in an emergency. You'd love it."

"You mean I need it," he said.

"Who doesn't? *I* need it."

"Maybe in a few weeks," he said, "a month. I promise. Right now it's going so well with the weights. Getting stronger fast—I love this feeling."

"Just take it slow, Ras, OK? Don't be impatient. Don't be all about the metrics."

"Me, impatient? Metrics?"

She'd caught him the day before, in her apartment bathroom, weighing himself for the second time in an hour.

"You don't want to leave this life crushed by a barbell," she'd added, "with Ariana Grande hiccupping through a vocal processor."

Now they kissed, lips warmly open. With a yoga mat rolled under her arm she disappeared through a cedar door into a dark-windowed room that from the outside resembled a large sauna.

He warmed up with some quick push-ups and sit-ups. Too impatient for static stretching, he selectively embraced the opinion of those experts who'd recently deemed it a waste of time. In the sunny, south-facing squat rack room he fitted plates onto a forty-five-pound bar and lowered it onto the floor for deadlifts. Back in the sprawling main room, he plated another bar on a racked bench for chest presses.

Wednesday's lunch hour was always the gym's slowest, and today, as luck would have it, the free-weights floor was almost empty. A few anabolic habitués hulked around, the older one flouting house rules as he always did by going shirtless, exposing the broad, hairless pectorals of an action-capture superhero. None of the gym staff in their logoed red sweatsuits ever bothered him; in fact, when he was up here, they rarely appeared at all, thus delicately avoiding the task.

Rasmus completed his first couple of sets of lighter lifts. Though the playlist was hardly audible, his brain, gravitating as always toward minor vexations, seized on an especially annoying line and started looping it through his inner ear: *Late night devil put your hands on me . . .*

He finished his first serious set of chest presses and racked the bar above his face. As he lay breathing, his eyes refocused on the screen suspended from the ceiling directly above and angled slightly floorward so it was visible from below. The sound was off. Closed-captioning in block caps, studded with the usual obvious misreads and typos, unscrolled while a hollow-eyed journalist reported from a sunny beach strewn with life jackets and perhaps—it was hard to be sure, and Rasmus looked away—human bodies.

Engaging his core, he sat up, stood up. He felt strong today. He walked into the sunny side room, executed a set of deadlifts, added weight, returned to the bench. Back and forth, set by set, as those mockumentary-grade lyrics wormed in his ear and the closed captions stock-tickered. Whenever he paused at the water fountain, his limbs, reflected in the wall of mirrors, looked more inflated and veiny, his face more flushed and relaxed, as if he were visibly aging in reverse.

The US president in a red baseball cap, prating and pouting for a crowd somewhere.

Video of hurricane winds tearing through palm trees, waves crashing over sandbag berms into small cubic houses.

Beside another mirrored wall, The Peach was setting up with her various kettlebells. Tia had coined the nickname with no apparent trace of sarcasm or judgment. In apricot leggings and crop top, The Peach would be performing deep squats and lunges for the next half-hour, her body in profile to the mirror, face turned to watch her backside pumping to the beat she must be hearing through her earbuds. By working her lower half exclusively, she'd grafted onto her skinny frame swollen fruit-like glutes that might have been silicone prostheses. She was the only person who'd entered for some time. Meanwhile one of the Action Figures had departed.

Near the end of the hour, Rasmus decided to do one extra set of bench presses, first adding a little more weight, a two-and-a-half-pound plate on either side. He promised himself he would stop at five reps, even four, instead of going for the full six. After all, who was watching?—aside from the usual internalized tribunal of judgers and scoffers, going back to early childhood. Tia had somehow exorcised that panel of phantoms, while he had simply learned to accept its presence, even to employ it for motivation. You could do worse, he reckoned. Tia sincerely believed that people could change; Rasmus was having none of it. You simply learned to work well with what you had. Which maybe amounted to the same thing.

He lay back and gripped the iron bar; Tia now was probably lying in *shivasana*. The captioning feature had malfunctioned, but he knew that the men onscreen, two white, one black, their suits snug over thick torsos, hands folded in front of them on a bar-like broadcast desk, must be discussing professional sports. As the men guffawed—heads thrown back, teeth gleaming in apex primate display—the captioning returned.

SOUND OF LAUGHTER.

He adjusted his grip, pushed up and unhooked the bar. It wobbled slightly. This was the heaviest he'd ever benched, twenty-five pounds over his body weight. But he let it down confidently, inhaling smoothly. He arched his back to meet the bar with his chest and then, soles braced on the floor, pressed up. His form was an untutored imitation of the regulars' style. The only thing he did not imitate was their shunning of the steel butterfly clips that lesser lifters used to secure the plates on the bar. He guessed regulars were expert enough not to need them. Or was it simply a way of showing off?

This first rep was already challenging. Slight trembling in one arm (oddly, it was his left, stronger arm), but he forced the bar to lockout and exhaled with a huff. A few specks of spittle launched screenward. Not wanting to lose momentum, he let the bar right back down. He would either finish after a second rep or, possibly, rack the bar and ask somebody to spot him for one or two more.

The shirtless, headphoned King of the Spartans stood over by the dumbbell rack, one grossly vasculated arm curling a toy-tiny weight. Like The Peach—who was still blasting out her squats—he was raptly tracking his efforts in the mirror.

Breathe. Bar to the chest. On the screen, two ranks of linebackers imploded and a quarterback, arm cocked, scanned the field, then drilled a pass toward the sidelines where a receiver stopped, pivoted and caught it. Rasmus pressed up. The bar moved slightly. He puffed hard as if to enlist his breath among the upward forces. The receiver, knees pumping high, was pelting downfield. The bar wouldn't budge. Rasmus shut his eyes, arched his spine and exhaled through locked teeth, pressing up with all his might. The bar rose an inch, then sagged to the left, that arm convulsing. He gasped a half breath, tried again. Now his right arm quaked and buckled and the iron shaft lay cold and heavy across his chest.

With the weight dead, his long arms pinned back, apply-ing real force was impossible. He glanced around the gym. No one had noticed. He gaped upward, tried to breathe, to gather his wits and strength. Onscreen a replay of something he'd just missed—the receiver bolting down the sidelines and colliding with a mascot in a grinning cow-horned costume topped with a Stetson. As if slipping a tackle at the goal line, the runner glanced off the mascot, dove and slid upfield, the ball clutched under his chest. The mascot was flattened, the Stetsoned headpiece flying loose.

Rasmus exhaled and pushed. No good. The 190-pound bar settled deeper over his emptied lungs. Cut to a replay of the accident from a fresh angle, then paramedics stretcher-ing the hurt man past an actual, enormous longhorn steer.

SOUND OF LAUGHTER.

The top of the man's head almost bald. Back to the sports desk, the trio shaking their heads and grinning.

He might have called for help at first, but with his lungs collapsed he could barely groan. He tried raising and wag-ging his head. *Here, somebody!* King Leonidas was still doing those light little curls. Under the pull-up rack a man with a samurai topknot was nodding down at his phone, thumbs twitching. He too had earbuds. Beyond him the Peach, gripping a kettle bell between her knees, was in her final phase, squatting deep, "ass to the grass," like a wasp trying to sink a stinger. Her frail arms wouldn't shift this weight any better than he could now. And it struck him. Why the

24

experts didn't use those clamps. Get trapped and you could tilt the bar just enough so the plates slid off one side and the imbalance would teeter the rest off you like a tipped scale.

Sweat prickled into his scalp and armpits; he smelled his antiperspirant and a trace of ketonic sweat. These cavernous, sanitized spaces usually filtered out all fleshly odours, like a funeral parlour visitation room. He tried to twist and tip the bar off him. Another blooper onscreen: a golfer on the sunny verge of a water hazard, set to chip the ball, alligator surging up onto the grass, golfer fumbling club and prancing backwards as if hotfooting over coals, gloved hands framing a terrified rictus.

How much time remained in the hour, Tia's *shivasana?* He glimpsed the clock peripherally. Four, five minutes? He was hardly breathing, wouldn't last. "Hey," he managed to squeeze out, "here!" Pressure kept building behind his eyes, his cheeks and ears burned, it was partly shame, he was going to die and he felt less afraid than embarrassed. It was not his life flashing before his eyes but his funeral—the strain on murmuring faces trying to maintain decorum as they skirted the irresistible weirdness of his death.

SOUND OF LAUGHTER.

Like a tourist gored by wild boar in the streets of Rome, a man flopping over a zoo railing into a baboon enclosure. Plus that added dollop of fatuity that always attached to midlife male vanity and striving, as with a love-hotel heart attack.

Poor Tia would find him. She who'd remarked that nothing in this culture was content to let people live in quiet, dignified self-esteem. This mishap would attest it couldn't let them die that way either...At last sheer terror volted out from his solar plexus through every particle of his being. At the same time desolation flooded him as if the prolonged pain of some heavy grief had been compressed into seconds. They'd met at a pharmacy magazine rack, she radiating well-being and equanimity against a backdrop of chagrined crowds under lurid lighting. In blue-rimmed glasses she was scanning the psych and science section, he with his hand on a hockey magazine. Momentarily their gazes crossed. He glimpsed his own hand sliding over and gripping a *Scientific American*. She chuckled under her breath, he glanced back at her, they cracked up in unison.

He pressed up furiously as if somehow he might have recouped energy, not hemorrhaged more of it, but then wasn't panic supposed to unleash superhuman strength? The young mother deadlifting the Toyota off her toddler... Ah, but that was for *love*. Does anyone love themselves enough to recruit that once-in-a-lifetime strength? Tia, maybe. She had done the work. She might say we all sometimes carry a weight across the heart—she saw it daily in her practice—that's enough to destroy you unless you get out from under it and start over.

Dying prey animals in nature docs always seemed to give up sooner than a person would, as if instinct cued them when further struggle would only prolong the pain. And for a second he got it—how acceptance, an ecstasy of relief and yielding, could well up and anaesthetize you. He stopped moving. On the screen, a haggard old couple sat meekly gratified as a fit woman in a skirt suit reassured them.

A PLAN FOR EVERY STAGE OF LIFE.

Reviving, he wriggled under the bar, raised his head and cast around: the samurai still thumbing, the king now curling with his *other* arm (how did he not notice the struggling figure behind him, reflected in the same mirror?).

Now Rasmus's squirming and arching made the bar slide down his sweat-slick breastbone toward his neck. He braked it just below his collarbones. If this were a bar fight and he were pinned on the floor, his bigger assailant was going for his throat. He locked his chin tight to the sternum, shielding the throat, and averted his face. The bar crushed into the left side of his jaw. Relax the chin even slightly and the bar would find that rift, pry it wider, slot down into the groove and choke him. This was just physics but felt cruelly personal. His one hope was to *use* gravity. No way to force the bar back up the breastbone—so bring it down over the chin, the face. Shoes flailing to grip the floor, he tried to wiggle down the bench and grind his face under the bar while pushing it the other way toward the top of his head. Cold iron grated over his sealed lips and, below them, the incisors. A moan escaped his lips. The bar mashed his nose sideways. There was a popping and he sneezed blood, tasted salt and ammonia. A firestorm flared in his visual cortex as the left eyeball was squashed down, then the bar was

27

grinding across his brow, sliding away and thumping onto the padded bench behind him.

Instead of lying there catching his breath, cautiously taking stock like the wounded creature he was, he jack-knifed upright, stood and staggered away from the bench. Snot-thickened blood drooled off his chin to the floor. His facial bones throbbed as if his skull had been unscrewed from a vise, his nose bubbled, his vision crossed. He glanced around: the others all continuing as before. How perverse and yet predictable that once his relief at surviving had crested—a matter of seconds—a fresh flood of relief, almost as potent, engulfed him: no one had seen his mistake, his failure.

The door of the yoga room swung inward. In a panic of vanity he glanced toward the mirrors. Beside the Spartan's pneumatically inflated, cranking arm, a slasher-film mask hovered: swelling eye, skewed, pulpy nose, mouth clumsily lipsticked with blood. The man dropped the dumbbell and recoiled from the reflection like the golfer retreating in the blooper reel.

Rasmus turned back. In the doorway Tia stood gaping, gripping the nape of her neck with one hand. Faces peered over her shoulders. She flung down her unravelling yoga mat and rushed over, both arms reaching toward the mangled figure Rasmus had just dimly, indelibly seen.

In the storm's-eye stillness of a world on pause, the silence seeming peaceful one minute, apocalyptic the next, he and Tia took to walking, sometimes for hours, on the city's ravine trails. He'd been about to return to the gym when the lockdowns hit.

That border between dystopia and utopia can be a slim one. On some outings they passed hundreds of other walkers, all suddenly furloughed from daily life and seeming less spooked than quietly pleased—while at the same time trying to play down their satisfaction. But then, most of these walkers were more or less affluent. Off-trail, the ravines were filling with rain-faded tents and tarpaulin lean-tos. The bridges that traversed the ravines were silent, almost devoid of traffic, yet away in the distance sirens howled constantly, nearing or receding. And Tia's clients were struggling more than ever; she, unlike most of these walkers, continued to work daily, sometimes still in person.

One April afternoon, the sun high and hot but the mature hardwoods still leafless, lending sightlines into the woods, something caught his eye. They were walking hand in hand, she as always on the inside, looking ahead, making eye contact with passersby and exchanging greetings, he looking down at the trail or into the woods. Middle-class politeness, she'd said, was partly a matter of self-congratulation, a community's ritual celebration of its status and security. "Well, then, why bother?" he'd asked, wondering if her public warmth was less sincere, more performance, than he'd believed.

"Partly it's for me," she said. "In a way it's an exercise, like meditation or any spiritual discipline. I don't always like people as much as I wish I did."

Now he stopped and, tightening his grip on her hand, stopped her. Not far off through the skeletal forest, a pair of black athletic shoes dangled in mid-air, swaying as if in a breeze. The day was perfectly calm. Sockless ankles and white, hairless calves extended up out of the shoes. The rest of the body was hidden by the densely needled boughs of a pine.

"Oh, no," he said.

He stepped off the trail and ran toward the shoes, calling back, "Wait there!" but she was with him, close behind, their steps crashing through the layered dead leaves. As he neared the dangling shoes and legs, they seemed to rise—maybe the optics of his swift approach? He swiped aside a wing-like branch of soft needles and entered a small clearing.

A lean-torsoed man wearing only green shorts and a backwards baseball cap was gripping the branch of a tree, close to the trunk, trying to chin himself. Young face, full beard. His eyes were strained shut, arms flexed and trembling. He jerked upward a few more inches and jutted his beard toward the branch, almost touching it, then let go and dropped into a squat in the soggy leaves.

After a moment he straightened up. His glassy eyes registered no surprise at finding two strangers present, their faces still cinched in grimaces of fear.

"Last set." He too was breathing audibly. "Oh, man, am I done."

"Glad you're all right," Rasmus said. "From the path we couldn't..."

Explaining might create an uncomfortable sort of intimacy, so Rasmus didn't. The man seemed to have no sense of what they might have misconstrued. Bending to pluck a T-shirt from the leaf-covered ground, he blew out a breath and said—as if anyone might be unaware—"Even gyms are closed. But it's not bad out here."

"No," Rasmus said, "beautiful. A beautiful day. We were just saying."

"Last set of push-ups now."

"We'll leave it to you," Rasmus jumbled.

"Wait." The man slid a smartphone out of his back pocket. "Could you get a shot of me doing one more? Or a ten-second video, for my channel..." He stopped, frowning down at the phone. "Not supposed to pass things hand to hand."

"I'll take it with mine," Tia said. "We'll send it to you."

"Cheers. I'm an influencer." He put down the phone and T-shirt and got back into position to jump for the branch, peering upward, hands raised and palms open, as if Tia had aimed at him not a cellphone but a gun.

As If
in
Prayer

The night shift at the camp had been quiet enough for sleep and the day broke mild and windless. I borrowed Tariq's scooter and rode ten minutes down the cliffside highway before turning inland onto a nameless, unnumbered road. I'd wanted a route that would avoid the larger towns while also taking me past a now-notorious landfill site; online images showed a pyramid of discarded life jackets whose immensity could be gauged only by the trucks parked at its base dumping fresh loads.

I rounded a bend and it loomed ahead, less impressive in reality even with sunrise lighting its thousands of orange-and-red facets like live coals. It was just a heap of garbage, after all. Many of the life vests were useless fakes, nylon shells that the human traffickers had stuffed with bubble wrap, boxboard, sawdust or rags. The fakes sold for ten euros in the markets of İzmir—six for the children's vests. I paused on the side of the road. After a minute I held up my phone, turned it for the wider view and fiddled with the zoom. I shoved it back in my parka without pressing the shutter button.

I rode on into mountains that were green with olive trees below the snow line and the bare summits. The road was empty. Looping upward, it gave views back toward the Aegean, tropically turquoise this morning and yet, as we all knew by now, cold enough to kill.

The first village I rode through was still shuttered and silent, as I'd hoped. I rode like a novice anyhow, stiffly upright, one hand shadowing the brake. My caution would have tickled any old men sitting out in front of the cafés, had the cafés been open. I'd driven no vehicle of any kind in just under two years.

The second village's main street—only street—was like-wise deserted, though a fragrance of warm bread was wafting from somewhere and, when I stopped to check the map Tariq had drawn for me, I heard the chugging of an olive press.

At first the authorities were burying the drowned in an old cemetery on a hill above the island's main port. By October they'd run out of room. They chose a new site, exclusively for refugees, near a remote mountain village where no tour bus ever ventured. It was this village I entered next. In the little gorge of the street, the Vespa's two-stroke engine made a nerve-shredding din. There was a time in my life when that amplified snarling would have excited me, made me open the throttle and delight in the speed-surge dragging me back on the seat.

Most hand-drawn maps are confusing and useless, but not Tariq's. As indicated, just beyond the village a dirt track veered left off the road. I took the turn, then bumped along through an olive grove, the old trees' bottom-heavy torsos fantastically burled. Their willowy leaves absorbed and deadened the scooter's chainsaw howl. The heavy black fruit was still unharvested.

I emerged into a clearing the size of a baseball field. Olive-treed slopes rose amphitheatrically around it. The clearing was studded with gravestones and there were open graves with little dunes of dirt beside them. A small car and an even smaller backhoe were parked on the edge of the clearing. Near them a man, his face and chest visible, stood in a grave.

He was watching me, the blade of his shovel frozen mid-air.

I cut the engine. The turned earth was too loose to support the kickstand, so I walked the scooter back and leaned it against a tree. One of the olives hanging in front of my eyes was so ripe that the skin had burst, revealing white pulp streaked with mauve. As I touched the olive, it fell into my hand. I put it in my mouth and tasted the bitterness of fresh-crushed oil and something harsher that seared and furred my palate.

I approached the gravedigger, crossing the morning shadows of a row of headstones. They were thin tablets of white marble, like the stones in war cemeteries—in fact, like the ones just across the straits from here at Gallipoli. Inscriptions in Greek with Arabic below. UNKNOWN MAN,

AGED 30?, # 791, 19/11/2015. The care and expense that the bankrupt authorities had put into the stones was a heartening surprise. Only the number signs, like Twitter hashtags, seemed to fall short on decorum.

I stopped in front of the small grave. Maybe the man still needed to enlarge it? He'd put the shovel down so that the shaft bridged the hole. In this mountain air and direct light, things leapt into clarity with surreal resolution. There were tiny nicks in the cutting edge of his otherwise new shovel. His broad-boned face, looking up, was sallow and freckled. Sun-marbled eyes behind steel-rimmed spectacles, the round lenses too small for his head. Trimmed black beard, no moustache. A black keffiyeh around his neck and, over the stubble of a buzz cut, a white skullcap.

I wished him good day and peace, thus all but exhausting my Arabic. When he replied in Greek, *"Kalimera,"* I automatically answered, *"Ti yineis"*—How's it going?—as if I couldn't see.

"Mia chara kai dyo tromares," he said, the *ch* sound rasping low and throaty, as in Arabic. *For every joy, two troubles*—a standard Greek response. He went on in Greek, "You're bringing news about more bodies on the way?"

"It was calm last night," I said. "Just five or six boats, maybe three hundred people. They landed wet and cold but all right. Not like last week, thank God."

"Sure, why don't we thank God? He has come to expect it."

I never said things like "thank God" anymore. I must have been trying to connect with the man; despite his track suit top, khakis and construction boots, I'd assumed he was a young Muslim priest or lay cleric. Probably, too, I'd meant to reassure him that I wasn't one of those hostile islanders who had lost jobs to the crisis.

I said, "I think your Greek is better than mine."

"Well, I've been here long enough." He explained that his name was Ibrahim, he was from Egypt, he had arrived in Greece ten years ago on a work permit. He'd stayed on as a labourer in Piraeus and eventually came to Lesvos for a construction job. In September—laid off like everyone else—he approached the authorities and volunteered to wash, shroud and bury the bodies of the Muslims drowning nightly in the seas between Turkey and Lesvos. "October was a very busy time, as you probably know," he said. "You are a foreign volunteer?"

"Yes, from America. It's Peter."

"Are you ill? You look as if you need to be sick."

The astringency of the olive was intensifying as it dissolved. I'd been wanting to spit, but I wasn't about to do it while he stood chest-deep in an unfinished grave, telling me about his life.

I talked around the stone, my mouth puckering: "I ate an olive. Off the tree there."

"Ah!" His white incisors shone cleanly, though the eye teeth were yellow. "You thought you could eat them right off the tree! Many volunteers make this mistake."

"No, no, I knew. I was here as a child, a number of times. We—my Greek cousins and I—we used to pick and chew olives, on a ..." *On a dare,* I wanted to say but couldn't remember the Greek phrase. "It was a game. We'd see who could last longest before spitting."

"Please, friend, spit now."

39

I took a few steps toward the dusty, dented car, hawked a few times, then toed dirt over the spatter of violet pulp. The car's hatch was half-open. An old Fiat Panda. As I walked back, the man lifted his hands and gazed around us: "A fine spot here, isn't it? As far from the sea as you can get on this island, or so the villagers tell me. For the sake of the people I'm burying, I'm relieved."

My lapsed Greek, along with his accent, created a kind of satellite delay; I was always a few words behind, and even when I caught up, I wasn't sure I understood.

"They're letting me stay in an abandoned house in the village," he said.

After a moment I said, "Yes, they told me in the camp, but I came straight out here to find you. I figured that after this last week, you'd still be busy."

Eight nights before, a rubber dinghy crammed with Syrian families had capsized a half-hour off Efthalou Beach. The people whose life jackets were genuine were pulled, alive or dead, out of the sea that night or the next morning. The ones wearing fakes had vanished, and then, after bloating and resurfacing, washed ashore.

But some of their belongings had washed up only yesterday.

"I did actually bring you something."

"Foreigners have never lived here before," he said quickly, "let alone a Muslim. Not since the time of the Ottomans. Two nights ago, we had snow."

I unslung my day pack and set it down by my boots. There was a splash of olive pulp on one toe.

"My little house feels a bit empty in the evenings," he pushed on, "especially now with the sun setting so early. Still, it's the first house I've ever had. You have a family, children?"

"Maybe someday," I lied. "I guess you don't, yet?"

"Now more than ever I'd like to. But what woman will have her children with a man whose hands have buried so many ...?"

No display of hands to emphasize the point. They hung slack at his sides. I crouched down and unzipped the day pack.

"I do wish they'd chosen a slope," he said. "A slope would be better at this time of year. Drier. I hate seeing water in the graves! Of course, trying to operate the digger on a slope ..." He kept speeding up. I was straining to follow. "I use life vests as pillows for them, between the sheet and the earth. For pillows, it doesn't matter if the vests are real or not, so long as they're soft."

Our faces were closer now that I was hunkered down. Faint acne scars on his cheeks above his beard. Behind his lenses, the eyes were intently fixed: the desperate gaze of a castaway.

I reached into the pack. The little rosewood box I'd brought here was swaddled in a toque and a hoodie. "Last week," I said, "we actually found a vest stuffed with ..." I didn't know the Greek for bubble wrap. He wasn't listening anyway.

"It's remarkable how efficiently the sea strips them," he said. "It wastes no time at all—and still it is not satisfied! Given a few extra days it removes arms, legs, more."

From the slopes behind him a voice, probably a goatherd's, was calling.

"This one I'm burying, her life vest was filled with——" (a word I didn't know—possibly bubble wrap?), "which of course is useless for anything *but* a pillow. Still, I won't be using it. Her body needs no pillow."

I was holding the box with two hands, watching his lips move above his beard, waiting for the words to resolve into sense. Resisting the sense. Grateful I was no longer fluent. "I'm sorry to bring you this," I cut in. "I don't even know what you should do with it." I snapped open the box. It might once have held earrings. The burgundy felt lining was stained darker where sea water had leaked in. Nestled on the felt, like pearls, lay three baby teeth that someone had kept—maybe the parents of a child who had died back in Syria, maybe a living child who had saved them and carried them aboard the raft.

"Bury it on its own, maybe?" I suggested.

"God, I suppose, is the only one."

I looked at him.

"Without a broken heart," he said.

I tried to ease the box shut, but the hasp caught with a click.

"I guess this must be a child's grave," I said.

"Of course, yes, I said so! An unknown child."

Ena agnosto paidi. I'd missed that whole phrase. I said, "And I guess it would be wrong to assume that these—that the box—is this child's?"

"Had she been the only one, maybe we could." He took the box from me. Held above the grave, it looked even

smaller, the sort of thing in which a child might ceremoni-
ally inter the husk of a cicada, or a dead mouse pup found
curled in a field. "Still, we should put it somewhere. And it
might be hers. Thank you for bringing it all this way."

"It's little enough."

"Yes, tiny, it weighs nothing."

"No—I meant it wasn't much to do. Not a long ride. Let
me help you finish here. I've been digging a lot at the camp."

"What—graves at the camp?"

"No." Extra latrines, I'd meant.

"This one is already bigger than it needs to be," he said.

They lay on a northwest-to-southeast axis, the graves,
bearing toward Mecca and the morning sun, the heads of
the deceased oriented as if in prayer.

"I can help you carry and put the body in," I said.

"Everything is being performed in accordance with the
tradition," he said. "So, 'by Muslim hands alone.' I am even
reciting the funeral prayer. To me, these things matter little
now, but to them, I think..."

He put the box in his track suit pocket. I got up.

"I understand," I said, relieved.

If I'd meant my little courier run as another crumb of
expiation, I'd failed. If I'd meant my service here on the
island as a larger penance, that too had fallen short. As had
"community service" back home, as had my suspended sen-
tence. I told him nothing about the accident, of course, the
details no more pressing for being mine. Maybe there is no
penance, only time passing. A child's death is a tragedy back
home, but a thousand deaths—if they happen here—are

just data for a churning news engine. Even the drowned boy in that famous photo: not a person but a figure surfacing, briefly triaged from the unnumbered and unnamed.

"Did you know that in certain places they bury people standing up, just as I am now? Of course, this hole"—he used the Greek for hole, not grave—"would need to be deeper."

The music of December in the islands was drifting down from the slopes: a melody of goat bells, a backbeat of oak switches slapped against branches to bring down the fruit. He was speaking to me again, more slowly. As if understanding, I nodded.

Wash her.

Water and . . . snow?

Home. Her home.

I bent down to shake his cool, dirt-seamed hand and wished him well.

As I gripped the scooter handlebars, I glanced back. He was holding the shovel, standing in the grave. I walked the machine out through the grove and by the time I reached the road, his last phrases—a prayer, one he would now recite in Arabic?—had settled into sense.

Wash her with water and snow and hail . . .
Give her a home better than her home.

Expecting

The calendar indicated spring, but the weather was equivocal and kept the city on hold. Steep sunlight, as yet unfiltered by any leaves, dazzled the eyes and burned the skin, but the winds were icy. A month of recidivist weather: tomorrow it might easily snow. Leonard and Halli Losco were driving home after their Sunday brunch in the Market—a ritual that had been central to their life together since they'd met four years ago, but which Losco suspected might soon be subject to suspension, or worse. Halli was due in two weeks and last night had experienced some preliminary cramping, a benchmark they'd learned about in the prenatal classes that had recently concluded.

"So here we go," Losco had said.

"Not yet, silly," she'd told him, curled on her side, her head on his shoulder while his eyes probed the ceiling, as if for hairline cracks. "I mean, it could be a couple more weeks, even more."

Losco as a child had been so anxious that, had he grown up three decades later, he'd have been well acquainted with therapists and would have swallowed medication with his morning juice. Instead, he'd painstakingly coached himself beyond his phobias and become—as his business partner, Vance, put it—cowboy calm. He was a bulky, plodding kid with black-frame spectacles and curiously abbreviated legs. Sitting very upright at his school desk, he seemed of average height, even a bit above, but when he stood up, his large head remained more or less at the same level and his true stature was revealed. This anomaly generated both merriment and creativity among his schoolmates, who called him Tiny Lessco, Lost-legs, and Legs-low, as well as Colossco, Moscow, and Loser Losco. More laconic peers skipped the preliminaries and simply shoved or struck him, though seldom with any committed hostility. Allusions to his ethnicity—he'd inherited the swarthiness and vaguely Semitic features of the Maltese parents who insisted on ferrying him to and from school each day—were less frequent and, when they came, oddly tentative. Possibly his schoolmates considered ethnic slurs superfluous given his physique, or else they didn't know how to go about disparaging the Maltese, who were not quite Wops, or Kikes, or Greasy Greeks, or Pakis, or anything else, and came from an island no one had heard of or could find on a map.

Then Losco chose Stendhal's *Le rouge et le noir* for his grade ten French project and was struck by its little hero's Napoleonic willpower. It hadn't occurred to him that you could so fully and plausibly concoct a new character for yourself, thus tightly regulating how others viewed you. Invisibility was not the answer after all. Nor was a class clown's ingratiating hijinks. Image management was the key. So Losco—constantly goading and grading himself—worked to perfect a quiet, wry, never-ruffled persona that his peers began to notice. At university he was widely admired and even imitated by men who, a decade earlier, would have despised or overlooked him, or noticed *only* his lower half, a condition he had not grown out of and continued to regret. Still, he was rarely anxious now about his physique or any other thing. His years of disciplined shamming had convinced his very core.

Halli was the sort of woman whose every step or gesture is a small calamity for any watching male—so Losco told himself, with pride. Slim and tall, she moved with effortless grace. Yet she seemed unaware of, or indifferent to, her charms. Her large brown eyes appeared wholly uncalculating—instead sympathetic and gently amused. She laughed often, though rarely at jokes. She lapsed easily into reveries or trances but in a moment could bear down and focus with tenacious practicality.

He had never been with a woman of such varied enticements and hardly a day passed when he didn't shake his head and marvel at this outcome. As for Halli, like women before her, she was drawn to his calmness, which read as uncomplicated male confidence and which he knew must seem all the more remarkable given his size and appearance. His one good feature, he believed, was the firm, stoical jaw he'd sprouted in his teens. With a replica straight razor he groomed it each morning, weekends included.

The irony was that once Halli entered his life, his boyhood anxiety began to creep back. The sensations: motion sickness without the motion; a slight but chronic tightness under the sternum; the unsettled pulse of a man constantly expecting final notice from a loan shark. In the bedroom there had been a few close calls and Losco, aiming to pre-empt serious trouble, had supplied himself with pharmaceutical fail-safes that in the end proved unnecessary.

Still, they'd been happy, often deliriously so—or so he believed, much of the time, when the anxiety was more or less in abeyance. But with the pregnancy it became worse, a flutter felt not just internally but around him, somehow, in the spaces of their house, like a faint tremor from a construction site. When he finally told her, she said in her sensibly upbeat way, "If you didn't feel even a tad nervous, *I'd* be nervous, love. It shows you're taking this seriously." He joked that he was just worried that their son—he'd insisted on the ultrasound—would inherit his stature instead of hers.

Odd how the return of unpleasant symptoms—so familiar despite their long absence—could also bring a trace of relief.

Driving them home now, Losco gripped the wheel of the car with hands at ten and two o'clock. The traffic was light, but his eyes flicked mirror to mirror, as if they were on the 417 at rush hour. He'd drunk too much of the restaurant's potent coffee and he could feel the pulse under his chin. A glossy metallic-blue suv loomed alongside, swung closer and then, as Losco tensed, veered away. Without signalling, it steered into a turning lane and then, too fast, onto an off-ramp.

Halli said, "What's that?"

From the corner of his eye he glimpsed something detach itself from the roof of the suv and fly off.

"What was it?" he said. "They hit a bird?"

She was looking back. "Pull over, Leo."

"What, here?"

"We have to stop, love."

"What *is* it?"

"I think a wallet. It's on the shoulder of the road."

"Or maybe a learner's manual. That idiot can't drive to save his—"

"Just pull over, Leo, OK? I think it's—"

"OK, OK, I'm pulling over!"

"I think it was on the roof."

He brought the car to a stop and reversed along the shoulder. The Audi A4 was a standard and he had driven it for eight years, tall in the seat, jaw heroically firm, eyes fixed coolly on the road in a way that several women before Halli had admitted they liked, trusted. He was backing up quickly, nearing the off-ramp.

"Oh, a car just drove over it! No, it's OK—they didn't hit it."

"Guy must have been filling up," he said.

She looked at him.

"In the SUV," he said. "Must have left his wallet on the roof. This is as far as we can go."

"OK—I'll go get it."

"What, are you kidding?"

"Love, I'm fine, I'm not in a wheelchair!"

"Let me go for it, Hal, OK? Please?"

He leapt out before she could argue. He walked back along the shoulder and looked both ways up and down the off-ramp—it was only one way, of course—then stepped into the lane to retrieve the wallet. He made himself move casually, transparently, nothing to hide from the few passing cars. Security cameras must be observing him too. For a moment he saw himself on video, a small, blurry figure stooping and reaching for some object. Maybe he should have let Halli get it after all? No one would ever suspect her of a nefarious deed—Halli, pregnant and with her usual bright aura of blamelessness, of exemption from the usual human failings.

He gave her the fat wallet and pulled back onto the parkway. She told him she would find some ID, a number to call. Her cellphone lay in her lap, inches from her distended belly (lately he'd been pestering her to keep it out of her lap and away from the baby). Looking through the wallet, she said, "We'll call him as soon as I find a number. If he lives nearby, we could take it right to him!"

The prospect of this little expedition—its novelty, its helpfulness—clearly pleased her. Something he'd noticed about his revived anxiety was that it pre-empted such generosities (not that they'd ever been his strong suit) by making him warily weigh every action, and by tilting him even further toward cynical suppositions. He was thinking now that the wallet was likely stolen, then gutted and left on a stranger's car roof, a clever way to dispose of it randomly.

"Any credit cards?" he asked.

"Three different ones. And a driver's licence, health card, SIN card—Jean-Denis Beaulieu, that's his name. Even his passport."

"His *passport*?"

"It's in the—oh, what do you call it—in the cash slot, with the cash."

"How much?"

"A twenty and a five. I'm still looking for a number. Wait, here . . . I'll call him, this must be his card. It's a video arcade in Gatineau."

"Really? I didn't think there were any of those left."

Peripherally he saw her lift the phone to her far ear, then cover the ear closest to him with her free hand, a natural enough manoeuvre, yet it set off a thrill of pain under his heart, as if she were trying to exclude him from some private exchange. Silence. Then she was speaking, apparently leaving a message in her flawless Parisian French. He knew many of the words and heard her leave her cellphone number and their home number, but, oddly, he couldn't make out the message's full import, though in context it should have been easy.

"I was hoping it was a cell number," she said, setting the phone back down in her lap, on top of the open wallet, "but I guess it's a land line. But he might check for messages once he figures out he's lost his wallet and passport."

"I would."

"I know you would, sweetheart." She said the words fondly enough, but then again, the line between settled affection and love's erosion in habit and predictability—was it not a fine one?

He pulled into their flat driveway, needlessly setting the parking brake, and turned to her. "Home."

She sat unmoving. These days, when the fatigue hit her, it was abrupt and flattening. For the last five weeks or so she'd been taking a long nap after their brunches. Gently, briskly, he relieved her of the wallet, then jumped out of the car and came around to her side.

As he unlocked the front door of the house, he glanced back across Cedar Street, which was cedarless, wide, no sidewalks. Murray Olson—a perpetually tanned, lanky widower in his seventies—raised a hand and left it aloft almost in the manner of a blessing. In his other hand Olson held the tall rake with which he'd been turning the earth, readying his garden. Halli irradiated him with a broad, spontaneous smile. No one besides Losco could have guessed that she was desperate to climb upstairs and collapse into bed for the rest of the day.

He disliked bringing the wallet over the threshold into their home, as if this step transformed a commendable act into a de facto theft. After tucking Halli into bed—promising her he wouldn't spend his whole afternoon trying to return the wallet—he went straight to his office, eased shut the door, and checked the home phone for messages. Nothing. He called one of the man's credit card companies. To his surprise he found that they would do nothing to help either him or Jean-Denis Beaulieu. The man on the line, Pardeep—strong Indian accent but flowing English—seemed astonished that Losco expected him to give out a customer's contact details. "But he's lost his *wallet*," Losco protested. "We have his card— he'll want it back, right? Can't you at least reach him and give him our number?" The wallet—square, black, metallically shiny—sat on his desk as it had on the road. He eyed it as if it were some improvised explosive device. "I mean, I really want to get this thing back to him."

The man said the company could do nothing until the customer contacted them.

"And *has* he?" Losco demanded.

"I cannot answer this question, sir."

Next he tried the police. They were no more helpful. They suggested he consider contacting them after twenty-four hours if he still hadn't heard from the owner of the wallet. He left a message at Beaulieu's work number, as Halli had done, though Losco recorded his in English. He keyed in the web address of the video arcade and crashed out a wordy email, more detailed than necessary, his fingers snapping over the keyboard. He flagged it urgent. Then he rifled through the wallet again—careful to replace everything exactly—but found no other contact number, though he did notice something that both Halli and he had missed so far. Several items were out of date: a debit card, one of the credit cards, also Beaulieu's driver's licence and Quebec health card. But the SIN card and passport were current. He rubbed his eyes, blinked moisture onto his contact lenses, and looked again at the passport photo: a man with the neck of a rugby tackle, a stubble beard, thick black hair that seemed to erupt from his scalp just an inch or two above the eyebrows. What no such image could indicate—and who understood this better than Losco?—was the person's size. Beaulieu might be anything from a giant to a burly dwarf. (Losco glanced again at the driver's licence, where an actual height was listed: 180 cm.)

An internet search turned up little information, just a few hits linking the man to the video arcade and citing that same phone number. Two other men shared his name, one of them deceased, the other a notary in Laval with a busy Facebook page.

Halli slept for three full hours. Since long before the pregnancy she'd enjoyed this happy capacity to sleep at any time. Losco saw this knack, which he mostly regarded with affection but at times also envy—even a trace of puritanical censure—as another sign of her healthy, feline nature. She did not live to one side of herself but wholly within her own being, her own instinctive life.

He was in his office, checking email again, when she came in.

"Leo—honey—I told you I'd deal with it. I *knew* you'd..."

"What?"

"Nothing, love. It's OK. So he hasn't called back?"

"Must be nuts. Hasn't he noticed his wallet is missing?"

"It's Sunday, Leo—some people don't check things as often."

He studied her face, half expecting something new to appear there, some expression he'd never seen before. He said, "It's just—I hate having this thing hang over us."

"Then we won't let it! Would just soup be OK for dinner? Maybe Thai?"

"Let me do it, Hal, I said I would."

"I've had a long rest, love. Let me, I want to."

And she withdrew before he could object. For a moment he felt he might lower his brow to his desk and weep. She loves me, she loves me, she loves me as much as I love her— and how can that be? And yet it seems she really does, still.

He turned to some of the work he'd meant to catch up on during her nap. He and his partner had an investment consulting firm and for a year Halli had handled the communications side of certain portfolios (she could calm and conciliate the prickliest clients), but lately, of course, she was falling behind.

The telephone on his desk detonated. "Hello?" he said in the cool, noncommittal bass he affected whenever answering.

Through a heavy accent—not French—a loud voice pushed out a word and repeated it. At first he thought it was a garbled *hello*, then he thought it was *Halli*, then, perhaps, *Ali*.

Losco said his own name, then, "Who am I speaking to here?"

"This is *Halli?*"

"Losco, Leonard Losco. Who is this?"

"She leaved me a message."

"Today?" The tweak of jealous suspicion came with a sense of familiarity, as if he felt it all the time or had long been expecting it; this could not be Beaulieu, surely; this was the eventual interloper who had always been destined to call.

"Of course, yes, today!" said the voice.

"What is this about?"

"What? You have my wallet, yes?"

Losco glanced at call display and scribbled down the number. "Please tell me your name."

"Jean-Denis Beaulieu."

Losco's own French accent was mediocre, he knew, but he himself could have pronounced the name more correctly.

"Would you rather speak French?" Losco asked. "I think I can manage. My wife's is better, but, uh, she's—"

"Halli?"

"Yes, Halli, my wife!"

"No, my French is no better than English."

"But—"

"My mother was not Québécoise," he said brusquely, as if he'd had to explain too many times. "I grow up elsewhere, Albania."

After a moment Losco said, "ok, well—so can you come pick this thing up? No, hang on," he said, hesitating to give their address. "I can bring it to you. Where are you?"

"No, I am not," the man said confusingly. "I pick it after dinner. Where is your house?"

It hit Losco that he couldn't be out delivering lost items this evening, he had to stay with Halli. "What time would after dinner be?"

"What? I am not sure. Maybe eight."

"Why don't we say eight p.m., then. I'll be waiting."

"Maybe I be a bit later."

"Please don't. My wife . . . she's not feeling well."

"Ah yes, I see," the man said, now sounding amenable, even sympathetic.

With a spasm of dread that Losco recognized as irrational, he gave their address and simple directions.

In the kitchen he found her seated on one of the shining stools by the new black marble island. She was hunched over, a hand spread over her belly, the other splayed on the marble. On a cutting board lay the chrome-bright Japanese chopping knife, tiny cubes of sweet potato, strips of bell pepper, veiny leaves of chard.

"Hal?"

"Don't worry. I'm fine. Just a little cramping. The soup's"—he finally took in the delicious aromas of chicken stock, coconut milk, lemongrass—"almost done."

"Let me take over. I knew you shouldn't be doing this."

"Oh, Leo, enough—I told you, I'm not a patient."

Firmly, but with a complete lack of vehemence—trusting as always that the world would listen to her with respect and, sooner or later, agreement—she'd maintained that the medical establishment had pathologized the natural process of pregnancy. Gradually she'd overcome his resistance to a midwife, though she had then compromised as well and agreed to have the midwife attend her not at home but in the obstetrics ward of the nearest hospital.

He wondered if he should be taking her there now.

She agreed to lie down in the living room and watch a little TV while he finished the soup and steamed some rice. She couldn't see him from the couch where she lay. He poured himself a Scotch from the supply he kept in the cupboard, for guests. She, of course, was not drinking while pregnant, and he had insisted that he would teetotal as well, in solidarity. He very much missed wine at dinner—and contrary to the forecasts of acquaintances, the craving did not fade. Most evenings now, after she turned in, he would serve himself a double, afterward carefully washing the glass and observing his hand—a stranger's, small and hairy—replace it in the cupboard.

Over their supper, after he'd filled her in on the phone conversation, she said she was curious to meet the elusive

Monsieur Beaulieu, but by eight thirty he still hadn't arrived and she said she couldn't wait up any longer. Losco kissed her at the foot of the stairs, then loaded the dishwasher very quietly, not wanting to miss the sound of the doorbell.

He went out onto the front porch and looked up and down the empty street. It was almost dark, but there was still a glow to the west above Olson's roof—a surface decidedly in need of repair.

"Where the fuck *is* this guy," Losco said in a gangsterly undertone that he was pretty sure would have shocked Halli.

At 8:55 he took a second Balvenie up to his office and called the number he'd jotted down. Two rings, then an answer, *"Allô?"* A background of white noise, the hum of a highway or busy street.

"Jean-Denis?" He hoped his gruffness would convey his feelings and spare him elaboration.

"Oui, c'est moi."

The tone was blunt and cold, acknowledging nothing.

"Leonard Losco here . . . Hello?"

"Yes, I am here."

"But you're not *here.*"

"Pardon?"

"You said you'd be here at eight!"

"At eight, yes. It was impossible."

"You're on your way now?"

"I think so."

"You *think* so?"

No answer.

Losco tried to fill his lungs, his chest suddenly tight. He said, "I'll see you shortly, then," and added, as if Beaulieu might have forgotten, "I have your *wallet* here." Silence. *"Hello?"*

The man had hung up.

By nine thirty Losco was in a full-blooded fury. What if he too had needed to turn in early? He snapped the laptop shut, having cleared out his inbox—a feat he tried to accomplish at least twice a month and which usually left him feeling cleansed and in command. He closed his office door, slipped downstairs, let out Halli's old cat, Mitch, then fiercely emptied and cleaned the litter box. Down in the finished basement he changed into his gym gear, switched the widescreen TV to a documentary channel and boarded the treadmill. His short, hairy legs chugged beneath him, adrenalin overriding the whisky. He felt he could easily run for an hour, and maybe he would—though surely Beaulieu would appear in the driveway before then? Losco would see him coming: the basement was dark except for the TV, while a grated window high in the wall gave a ground-level view of the lawn, the driveway, and Olson's house across the street.

Olson's upstairs light winked out. It was after ten. *Blameless Bastards,* Losco was joining the documentary a bit late, followed an Irishman's search for his elder half-brother, taken as a baby by the Church from its unwed mother a few years before she married and went on to have a "legitimate" son. On her deathbed, she'd told this son that his half-brother had been raised by nuns in a special home. The son's search had revealed that thousands of children like his brother had died in these homes, often of minor ailments—"an outcome bespeaking neglect"—and that while death certificates had been issued, few graves could be found.

Programs of this sort could be counted on to sharpen a workout. The angrier Losco became, the more he took it out on the machine, pounding the conveyor belt with his shoes while panting retorts and epithets at the TV. He'd rarely gone to church as a child. His parents had been conservative and traditional in most ways, but for reasons that Losco never managed to learn, they attended mass only at Christmas and Easter.

At 10:50 he stepped off the treadmill, towelling sweat from his sheared, balding head, and stood watching the screen as a voice-over described the discovery of some thirty tiny skeletons in an old septic tank behind a nunnery west of Dublin. Across the screen flashed images, thankfully low-res, of the grisly excavation—or was it Losco's sudden tears that made them look indistinct? "Sooner or later all buried wrongs must face the light of justice," the narrator intoned, and Losco in a thickened voice snapped back, "Yeah, right, tell me another good one!"

At 11 p.m. sharp—a touch calmer after the exercise—Losco called the number again. After four rings a recorded voice mumbled something about not being available ... *pas disponible*. He called back and listened more closely to the recording. No invitation to leave a message or call-back number.

He showered quickly in the basement washroom, so as not to bother Halli, then dressed and ran back up the two flights of stairs on his toes, silent. In his office he checked the phone for voice mail. Nothing. His email inbox was already clogging up again—spam, a few auto-replies, social media site invitations—but nothing from Beaulieu. He slid the bedroom door open and peered in. She was sleeping quietly. He ran downstairs and stepped out the front door in his slippers, then walked to the end of the driveway and looked up and down the street. The wind had died; the air felt milder than out in the harsh sunlight this morning. He looked back at the house to confirm that the street number was visible under the carriage lamp, as if the pruned juniper by the door could have sprouted a few feet higher since dusk. His eye was drawn up to their bedroom window and a memory seized him, not of real life but of a film he had seen years ago. An old farmhouse is turning on its occupants, a family. The father is outside at night, doing something—patrolling the grounds? No—there's an axe in his hands—he's chopping wood. He looks back at the house. In the high window of the room where his children lie sleeping, the face of some monstrous creature glows, staring out at him.

He went inside and phoned again and this time left something after the beep, a gruff repetition of their address. Haltingly he added, *"Je vous attends avec impatience,"* though as he hung up it came to him that the phrase actually meant something quite affable, "I look forward to seeing you," or even, "I can't wait to see you."

He took the wallet downstairs and sat on the couch in the front room, facing the street, curtains open. On a table beside him were a telephone, his glass of mineral water and another Balvenie, just a taste. The wallet's contents he emptied onto his lap. This time he noticed that Beaulieu was smiling slightly in his passport photo, one corner of his mouth curled up, which was odd, in fact astonishing—the bureaucrats at Citizenship were notorious for rejecting photos betraying even a flicker of a smile. Born Montreal, 1975. Customs stamps indicated that he'd visited Albania several times in the past few years.

The telephone rang and he swept it up.

"Yes?"

A phrase in that surly, Slavic-sounding French.

"Could you repeat that in English? Is this Beaulieu?"

"Are you still waiting me?"

"Of course I am! Do you want your wallet tonight or not?"

"What?"

"It's past eleven now. It's eleven thirty-*five*. Do you want your—"

"I cannot come there yet. I am very busy. I will come there soon."

"You're not serious."

"I am not... what? I will be there no later than one."

"One in the *morning*?"

"What...? Of course."

Losco heard himself babbling into the mouthpiece. "Forget it. OK? I'm going to bed now. I've got to be up first thing tomorrow. It's almost *midnight*. I'll stick your fucking... I'll leave your property in the mailbox and if it's still there tomorrow I'll be leaving it with the cops. The police— you understand?"

"You cannot do that."

"Oh, I can't? What can't I do?"

"You are meaning, the box for mail, outside?"

"Where else?"

"But you have my passport."

"I don't *want* to have your passport, ок? I want to give it *back* to you!"

"But, maybe someone steals."

"From my mailbox in the middle of the night?"

I should never have given him our address, Losco thought. Should have taken the thing straight to the cops.

"I tell you, I come there soon. Maybe before one."

"Look in the mailbox, then. I'll be asleep." Hardly. Losco knew his own nervous system—he would be alert for hours unless he took a sleeping pill, a practice he was resisting lately, since at any time he might have to drive Halli to the hospital. "Don't mind the barking of our dog," he heard himself add, conjuring a second, more formidable pet. "He can't get out at you."

"You cannot do this—I tell you this."

"Oh, you *tell* me this? I'm waiting ten fucking hours here and you tell me what I can or can't do?"

"Honey?"

"Just a minute," he said, and covered the mouthpiece. "Halli? Darling?"

"What's going on down there, Leo?"

"Nothing, Hal." She must be at the top of the stairs—yes, there. "Go back to bed, Hal, I'll be right up."

"I'm cramping again. I think maybe it's happening! I'm really wet."

"What, you mean your water broke?"

"I don't know, maybe. I just woke up. Oh . . . I've got to sit down."

"I'm coming, Hal!" He unblocked the mouthpiece and said softly, like a philanderer ringing off in a rush, "I've got to go." The line was dead. Onto the table beside his unfinished drink he tossed the gutted wallet and the various cards and passport, then leapt up and ran to the stairs. She was sitting at the top in the white linen slip she'd been wearing to bed this third trimester. In the half-light her eyes looked small and red, her lips tight.

"I'm phoning the midwife," he called up firmly, as if expecting opposition. "She'll meet us there."

"Wait . . . it might be easing off."

He took the stairs two at a time and sat beside her, put his hand at the base of her spine, kissed her clammy cheek.

"Come on, beautiful. I'll help you get changed."

The phone rang. He swore, startling her, and she flinched as if at another contraction. He leapt up and made for his office, calling back, "Sorry—just a sec!" He closed the door behind him and swept up the receiver. "What?"

"You hang up on me."

"You hung up on *me*. Now leave us alone, I've got to take . . ." He caught himself; he'd almost revealed that the premises might soon be empty. "I've got to get some sleep. I'll put your wallet outside now. Don't ring the bell when you come—I won't answer the door."

"But I come *now* to the door!"

"You've been saying that all fucking day! And I've let the cops . . . I've told them I've been trying to reach you—to return your property."

"Leo!" he heard.

He rammed down the receiver. "Just a second!" he cried, then plucked the receiver back up and called the midwife, Simone—he'd put her number on speed-dial—and asked her to meet them at the hospital. Then he grabbed his car key and his own wallet and strode out of the office.

He held her small suitcase as he opened the front door for her. She was supporting her belly with both hands, hunching over enough that she and he were almost the same height. Her eyebrows were crimped as if from the pains—or maybe fear, though she showed no other sign of it. As he locked the door, the land line rang from both his office and the living room. "Forget it," he said roughly, as if to Beaulieu.

He helped her into the front seat of the Audi.

"Leo? It's OK. We're going to make it just fine."

"I know that! Do you have everything?" It hit him that he was forgetting something himself. His cellphone? Yes. It didn't matter, she had hers.

"Honey," she said, "you want *me* to drive?"

As he neared the end of their street, trying to accelerate smoothly, reasonably, a white cargo van sped past them in the other direction. A street lamp's glare on the van's windowless side briefly showed the ghost of some painted-over name and logo.

"God damn it! I knew there was something."

"What?"

"Nothing," he said through his teeth.

"Leo, I need you to be calm now, for me."

"I know. You're right."

There was little traffic on Carling, and the lights, to his surprise, favoured them. He'd looked forward to this trip, brief though it would be; he'd planned to shine as her imperturbable pilot, guide and guardian. Now it seemed almost too easy. Something must be wrong, or about to go wrong. Some of the signage in this familiar strip now seemed charged with ominous significance, EMERGENCY STAIN REMOVAL, while ahead in the night the hospital's glowing H reared like a prophetic initial.

"Almost there," he said.

A red light finally stopped them. Her cellphone rang in her purse.

"Leave it," he said.

"Could be Simone," she said in a pain-flattened little voice. "Wait—this number. I think it's the wallet guy. I forgot about him. He didn't come for it?"

Losco stared ahead at the light. "Never showed."

"They're getting really close, the pains."

"We're there, Hal. There it is. Look."

"Oh!" she said. "Did you remember to bring Mitch in?"

"Damn it!" He slammed the base of his palm on the wheel as the light changed. "I forgot—I forgot the cat too!" They lurched forward with a roar. Among all the apprehensions bearing in on him now, worst was the old assumption that at some point, under some unforeseeable, fatal pressure, the elaborate device of his persona would crack.

In this part of the city, moving up meant moving down the slope, toward the Ottawa River, Westboro Beach and the "village." Two years after Oliver was born, they found a larger, slightly older house, a close stroller-push from the shops and the shore. If they were going to have a second child, they would be needing more space, they'd agreed, though for him there was another, more visceral reason he kept to himself: the first house had never felt fully secure after the night of his son's birth.

In the second house one night—Halli lazing on her side, her head on his shoulder, her mouth by his ear (she disdained the protocol confining women to certain awkward post-coital postures while trying to conceive)—she said, "You never did hear back about that wallet, did you?" It seemed this latest try had reminded her of the day leading up to Oliver's birth.

When Losco had driven back from the hospital at six the next morning, to let in the cat and feed it, he had found neither voice mail nor email from Jean-Denis Beaulieu. The wallet and its contents lay on the side table beside his unfinished Scotch and the lamp left on, forgotten in the scramble of their leaving. Curtains wide open. In his relief that no disaster had come to pass—the thug-faced Beaulieu smashing a window, breaking in, trashing the place, maybe finding and hurting Mitch; above all, Halli coming to some harm in childbirth—he'd sunk into the couch and plunged his head into his hands, shaken by sobs that were both violent and soundless.

On his way back to the hospital, from which he would bring his family home that afternoon, he'd dropped off the wallet at the police station.

"No," he says now in a tone of mildly intrigued surprise, as if the oddness has only just struck him. "I never heard anything more from the cops or that guy."

Their marriage is young enough that he can still remember every lie he has told her, and this is one of them. The truth: A few days after their return from the hospital, groping in the mailbox, irritably trying to dig out a flyer clinging to the inside, he found something he must have missed for several days—an old parking ticket, not his. On the back, someone had written a line with a failing ballpoint pen, the strokes almost slicing through the paper so that even where no ink had flowed, the message could be read:

YOU FORGET ME BUT NEVER I FORGET YOU

The words froze his nape and scalp and made him look up and around the quiet neighbourhood, as if someone must be watching the house, had been stalking them for days. Murray Olson waved from the garden where he was digging. Losco calmed himself. Nothing had happened, nothing was going to happen; Beaulieu had his effects back by now; he must have hacked out this note in a moment of balked fury. Losco crushed the note in his fist and buried it in his pocket, though that evening he removed it, flattened it carefully, reread it several times, then tucked it in a fold of his wallet, where it would remain secretly, dangerously, like an adulterous note he couldn't bear to destroy.

Professions
of
Love

S ome will attest, many, in fact, that I am one of the finest in the field. I can quote from grateful testimonials. I have received citations and awards from each of the three professional organizations to which I belong. I am surgeon of choice for many of this city's, this country's, most prominent and preferred names. I am said, actually, let me be frank, to be *the* finest in the field. Numerous colleagues have said this. Many of my patients have said this or would say this if they were asked. I could quote from some of their grateful testimonials, because, frankly, I do reread them. You may ask why I do this. I am fifty-six years old and in health and by any measure of these matters "successful." At the pinnacle of my practice: the top of my game. Well-to-do, one must add. Enveloped with honours. Or: embalmed with honours? Is that possibly the problem? That I feel I have nothing to strive for anymore? No *défi?* I prefer the French, my mother's language, my second of five tongues, a form of German being the first, *défi,* for challenge, in the sense of the World offering defiance, resistance. Which one duly tackles with zest. No, that is not the problem. No lack of zest. The ennui of arrival at the pinnacle is not the problem. A trite malaise of middle age. "Is that all there is" and so forth. No. Forget this. I like being here at the pinnacle. At the pinnacle it is thrilling and the thrill does not jade. Nor am I a man for whom self-assurance, like a slowly accrued encrustation of diplomas and titles and press clippings and social compliments and admiring looks and so forth, is a superficial phenomenon. Thin gauze, let us say, in constant need of reapplication, laid over a wound leading inward to a profound abscess of uncertainty. I do have uncertainties, but they are peripheral. Or, to rephrase the fact, not of my very essence. Always I have had this self-assurance. Just why, you may ask, I do not know. Even in childhood, yes, this superior assurance, albeit I was not especially large or powerful or fast, those boyhood prerequisites of status.

Never mind boyhood and its tedious clichés. This is about recent events. I have uncertainties, as I have said, but at the marrow of my character, no. My wife is leaving me. You are familiar with the adage that no man is a hero to his wife. I believe that the phrase actually runs: No man is a hero to his valet. The point is identical. I wonder if my wife has been the reason I have felt compelled, now and then, to reread public testimonials on my work, press clippings, even the private letters I occasionally receive from patients. To be sure, these have lent comfort when, now and then, I felt insufficiently appreciated, as everybody, of course, occasionally must. What I feel now, however, is a species of "grief":

a process, one reads, with many steps, "anger" being a station of the cross on that Calvary, though I seem not to have reached it, or to be in the vicinity. I never have been the sort to bear malice or make a long-term patient of my grievances, doctoring them along to sturdier strength, I am not obsessive in that way. I have always been an untroubled sleeper: though not at this moment particularly. Bafflement, I believe, trudges up that path alongside grief. In a sense I did act contrary to her wishes, but my motives were benign. I went against her wishes in the way that a man may go against a wife's wishes in arranging, say, a surprise party on her behalf when what she wants for her birthday, she has said, is to go out with him to their favourite, say, Greek seafood restaurant. Duly promising to take her to Molivos, secretly he ploys to "deny" her wish. The party is a gift that supersedes his promise while *surpassing* her wish! His motives are the motives of generosity, love! If he is especially thoughtful, he will have the party catered by Molivos.

She is four years older than I. A beautiful woman aging, on the whole, less well than she might be aging, and in that expedited fashion of a woman after her change of life. We have been married for twenty-nine years. Two sons, twenty-two and twenty, grown and now departed, attending the same university, Duke, in the United States of America. So mostly we have had each other to ourselves for the last two years. This has gone less well than one might have foreseen. For the first time we have been obliged to rehearse a long future conducted with no one for company but each other. She said, at first, that she was content, happy at the prospect.

The prospect troubled me! For the first time in many years, it seemed, with the haze of harried parenthood cleared away, I was able to look at her seriously. It seemed that she, or someone, something, had applied to her face the pancake makeup of mortality. I would have liked to suggest, diplomatically, that things might be done. How odd if the wife of a dentist should sport disintegrating incisors! Absurd for the mate of a fashion designer to attend social functions in a fretworn housedress redolent of naphtha! And so forth. Nothing would have been easier than to perform some simple work. I had been dropping, let me speak frankly, mild hints, from time to time, for a number of years, hints that she seemed not to detect, or decipher: or which possibly she chose to suppress. I stopped doing it. Listen. For a number of reasons that do not matter here, reasons of ethical principle mainly, albeit also, to be frank, of personal biography, having to do with my extremely divorced parents (both now happily buried), I would like very much to stay married to my wife. To use the common phrase, she has been a lover and a friend. Or the common terminology: supportive, loyal. If consistency and discipline have helped gain me success in my professional life, I try also to be consistent in my personal life. And I love Fidelia. There has been no other woman save Fidelia since my twenties. Surely I have looked at other women, you think, you ask, in my mind disrobed and dishevelled other women, since my marriage in April of 1980, pleasantly dishevelled them, yes, to be sure I have, on the street and in restaurants and galleries and at social functions I have spied them and, of course, in my operating theatre, there above all, I have scrutinized women with an intensity of focus which most men, I think, could barely conceive of. It is my *job*!

Too many of my colleagues call themselves, in private or, sometimes, in public, Artists. I refuse to do this. It is pretentious, in many ways. In certain ways. At least, many feel it is pretentious. Then again, does it simply, I wonder, restate the obvious, the *actual,* as a vulgar boast? For there is, come to that, a trace of truth to the claim. The canvas on which one works, the clay in which one works, is the face of the patient, of the women (and, increasingly, men) who come to one, many of them aging, of course, but some of them young and lovely, many in the performing arts, of course, others who are merely, who can blame them, vain, and wish to anticipate the attritions of time and one's many cares and that unacknowledged devil, gravity. Others are merely neurotic. These patients have been under my power, not to mention, often enough, a thorough anaesthetic, and I have never once, what is the phrase, "abused power." The profession is not without temptations and this one most evidently. *To exploit the patient's potential obsession with her doctor.* This is common wisdom. Psychoanalysis provides a word, not to mention a vast literature, on the subject. And it should know! To the patient, however, I am no mere psychoanalyst-father-figure, and certainly no ordinary doctor. An ordinary doctor can, with luck, by forestalling death, slow time. *I reverse it!* The effects of a skilfully conducted, successful operation can seem, frankly, almost preternatural, even to the surgeon himself: and after the fact, I have never once taken advantage of any patient's unconscious perception of me as, how shall I put the notion, more than merely human.

Of course, I was lucky enough to *love* my wife through all those years, not merely to be attached to her in the dry canons of the law. So the temptations of beauty, whether intact among my secretaries and assistants, or revised upon my table (these latter, of course, being the most tempting, for readily imaginable reasons well-explored by myth and classic literature!), were resistible. But in the two years since our younger son left home, my resistance has weakened. Finding myself day by day less drawn to my wife, who appeared to be drying up before my eyes, as if, almost, my eyes themselves were inducing these changes, I began to suggest more frequently and firmly that she should allow me to help her in the way that I had helped so many strangers before. Such a procedure would of course be "unofficial": the profession naturally "discourages" practitioners from performing on spouses, which is not to say that such things do not occur, they DO, and no doubt more commonly than I, who can cite several collegial instances, can attest.

Exactly what needed to be done was obvious. Nothing especially drastic. There was nothing specially unique about the ways in which age was affecting her, there never is. Around the eyes, the lips, the jowls, that horribly graphic noun, and the delicate skin of the throat. What concerned me was my own growing sense of, yes, almost, sometimes, *revulsion,* when, all right, *whenever* I would sit down to dinner across from this rumpled imposter, or wake in the morning beside her. I never had been able to persuade her to train herself to sleep on her back, to prevent pillow wrinkling around the eyes. A practice on which I had instructed countless patients. *Lie like a corpse to avoid looking like one.* I never used, of course, this dire motto by way of explanation: a quip of the profession, there are many such. In fact, I knew enough of my wife's character, how could I not after so many years, to realize that she was disturbed by my suggestions, and so I abstained from further such, albeit with an accruing sense of concern.

For my desire to help her was a matter of loving pragmatism, yes, as opposed to reckless idealism (I wonder if there is any other kind?). I could not *prevent* myself from feeling unattracted to this increasingly unrecognizable flatmate; I *did not want* to abandon her; I had the *means* and the *expertise* to remedy the trouble. Yet I knew she would be resistant. After all, her utter lack of vanity was one of the things that had drawn me to her years before and had kept us together since! In my profession, I am of course constantly exposed to vain characters, persons truly steeped and mulled in their vanity, mobilized by vanity, fully *indentured* to vanity. How refreshing, for all those years, to come home to a woman who was naturally beautiful and hardly seemed to know it or to care! She wrote about food for various prominent publications and I happen to know that when speaking to the editors of certain of those women's journals, she could be rather evasive about my profession. *I hated that!* She herself often voiced certain cavils and caveats about the profession, especially as the nature of my work changed over time. Yes, changed. In the early years, I worked mainly to rectify congenital defects, such as cleft palates, or to help recast the faces of burn victims. In time my reputation grew. Times were changing, as they always are, and increasingly patients approached me for "merely" cosmetic procedures, and this came to seem my métier. I had a capacity in that line, perhaps because, as I used to compliment Fidelia, I had the model, the matrix-plate, the Ur-mould, the form and very armature of natural beauty at home to work from.

My wife was not pleased by the direction my career took or by the new constituency of my clientele, which, admittedly, included certain unsound persons, like the lady who always petitioned me to give her toy terrier, too, "a little nose job," so that owner and pet should more perfectly resemble each other, but I believe that Fidelia, like me, is conjugally stubborn, determined to "hold things together" both for the benefit of our sons and out of regard for the life we have had together, the past, the present, the future. (In our favourite Greek restaurant, on the menu among other charming illiteracies, appears THE FUTURE OF THE DAY: one of our favourite shared jokes. Squid, typically.)

We love each other even more than we did at the start. Yes, despite my occasional, perhaps I put it too strongly, revulsion. Yes, and yet in certain lights. The light of breakfast assuredly. I will prepare the coffee with a traditional hand grinder while she sits at the table, the tabby, Familiar, in her lap. I love her inextricably. But a disjunction has entered, had entered, my regard. I yearned to correct it. My physical attraction to her, my lack of it, had fallen out of proportion to the love I felt. For if she had changed with age, so had I! Professions amend one. *Mine had made an invidious critic of my gaze.* My heart embraced her; my eyes poked and prodded. I felt cloven against myself. It made me think too much. Too much thinking is the death of marriage. I would end up leaving her, sleeping with other women, as other Swiss-German fathers, let us say a Certain Swiss-German Father and leave it at that, have done, for they, these women, are so readily available, avid for the deft, silver-haired Inverter of Time, and I knew that, should nothing change, *I would leave my Fidelia.*

Increasingly these were my thoughts in the weeks before the incident and its aftermath. Fidelia had seemed troubled, preoccupied for some time, she has always been prone to seasonal depression, and our annual holiday, this year in Belize, had helped little, perhaps because I was helplessly, visibly attracted to the mermaidenly younger women around us. Mentally disrobing them was of course unnecessary. I tried to disguise my ogling. This never succeeds. She tried to disguise her distress. Nor does this. I tried harder. I knew that I was causing my Fidelia pain. Near the end of the holiday, slowly wandering the beach alone, having left her napping, I saw an attractive woman, her back turned, rise out of the water in a corona of spray, hair fetchingly disturbed by the sea, and as I waded into the shallows to draw closer, a helpless satellite, the woman turned toward me and the jarringly aged face, framed, I now saw, with greying hair made darker by drenching, was *Fidelia's:* a face that did not belong on that body, which of course is exactly the case with her, she is naturally slim, stays fit with little regimentary exercise, has the legs of a woman twenty years younger. I believe that as I recognized her, she saw the enchantment die on my face, and in that instant of several linked deaths she saw everything.

In March, amid mild depression, Fidelia suffered a minor cerebral ischemic event. Initially it appeared to be a stroke of greater seriousness, but her condition stabilized within hours. A very minor stroke, the doctor, the medical doctor, diagnosed: more a warning than an actual stroke. He predicted that the minor lateral numbness that she continued to suffer at unpredictable times would diminish, and it did, that her right hand would soon recoup its full and considerable strength of grip, and it did, that the slight but discernible downsag at the outer corner of her right eye and her lips would correct itself within a few weeks, and it did not. By August he had revised his prognosis in regard to these latter asymmetries. They would likely be permanent. *She could have them surgically corrected, however.* Life, of course, is more or less a textile of such ironies. I have often wondered, why? I now believe that it must be owing to the quality of our attention, how our fears and fascinations (every fear is a fascination!) seek to materialize, the Unmanifest willing its own manifestation. How everything longs to come to life.

After waiting for another month to see if there would be any detectable improvement, during which time the asymmetries seemed, if anything, to grow more distinct, Fidelia, to my surprise, chose to have something done. Once she had made the decision, her attitude vis-à-vis the procedure was uncharacteristically impatient. The minor cerebral ischemic event had made her rethink many things. She was exercising more conscientiously. In every way she had grown more prudent about her health. I believe she was coming to regard Time, as I have come to regard Time, as I have perhaps always regarded Time, as the ENEMY it is. Not that I believe it to be defeatable! Only neurotic fools and faddists believe as much, or pretend to believe so, and I am neither neurotic nor faddist: nonetheless I feel that a certain, what, a certain *honour* lies in fighting a losing battle with courage and resolution, undertaking a *défi*, for what is life, after a certain point, but a rearguard action, a tactical withdrawal, for that matter what is every face I freshen but another recruit in this campaign against a predatory, insatiable opponent that seeks to strip us all of our dignity and our future, our grip on consciousness, our creaturely delight! Perhaps, then, I am more soldier than artist. Or: I am both at once. Or, in Fidelia's case, a suitor, one whose rival is mortality itself, and who will not simply step aside as his rival marks her as his own.

In the week before I operated, in September, I made no suggestions that, while she was under the anaesthetic, I could do *more* of the work that I had, in my mind, been rehearsing, revising, rethinking, *perfecting* now for some years. I kept waiting for her to ask me to undertake this, what, this "supplementary work." She said nothing! Of course she would say nothing: having declared herself contrary to the enterprise for so long, what could she have said but nothing, albeit certainly, knowing my feelings on the matter, she might have been expected to speak out *against* such work! Her silence, then, led me to suspect *that secretly she might well want something done,* but did not know how to ask! Pride would prevent it. Or call it, paradoxically, "vanity"!

I made love to her the night before the procedure, of course. "Of course," I add, albeit the act had occurred rarely enough over the preceding two years, especially over the preceding months. I was gentle and I comforted her, I was capable, in the darkness, of feeling the old familiar passions, *ja,* in the darkness where her body felt much the same as it had always, while her face in the dark was simply a face in the dark. Some married people, we are told, make service of the darkness as an aid to fantasy, so as to pretend that the husband or wife in their arms is not their spouse. *I used the dark so as to pretend that she was!* This poignantly evolved preference, for darkness over the light, for blindness over vision, what was this if not another loss of dignity for us both, the latest reverse in the unwinnable battle against Time, a dry run for that eventual, conclusive darkness and terminal anaesthesia. Nevertheless on that night my desire was immense, the blind orgasm coldly numbing my scalp, like, yes, a local anaesthetic, clawing a cry from me that scarcely sounded like my own. Hers was quieter, yet she clenched me with all her limbs as if to grip the life out of me.

Afterward, I told her not to worry. She was not worried at all. Her breath smelled of hunger as she said the words, she had had to fast since noon, of course, because of the coming anaesthetic, and yet, despite the presumed discomforts of this fast (Fidelia being a woman who loves to eat), she fell asleep long before I. As I lay there, I remembered a particular occasion from years before, when our younger boy, Oskar, either hearing our sounds or seeking some nocturnal comfort, perhaps a glass of water, entered the master bedroom. Finding Fidelia aboard me, sitting up, her hands gripping my head, fingers in my hair, which was then longer in the style of the time, while I groaned as if being injured, he called out with a truly heartrending sincerity: Mama, please, he didn't mean it! He didn't mean it, Mama, please...! When I did eventually sleep, I dreamt of a cat, bony, starved, not our pampered Familiar, lying on its side on the bed mewling with some grief it was of course helpless to articulate. In the dream, nonetheless, I felt this grief as my own.

The work on her right eye and the right side of her mouth proceeded quickly and with no complications. Amina, my anaesthetist, who had never actually met Fidelia before, as she, Fidelia, never came to the office, asked, at one point, I do not recall exactly when, if there was another patient booked in before noon. She had thought, she said, that I had cancelled the other pre-noon surgery. (I had.) She was puzzled, I think, because I was working quite fast, as if we were short of time, whereas in fact I was merely eager to get through the preliminaries on Fidelia, albeit I was of course working carefully and was only able to finish the work rapidly because my concentration was so acute, so engaged, so *instigated*, almost as if I feared Fidelia might regain consciousness too soon (impossible), or was it simply my excitement at being embarked on a task for which I had so long prepared myself in imagination, in phantasy? Then again, I always have felt hurried, feel that time is so short, a fact which, I believe, any truly vital being must believe: an eighty-year lifespan is a mockery of human dignity and potential, an "intelligent" and "curious" person could live three times that length without ennui or loss of direction. I believe this although Fidelia, strangely, never has, or had, agreed with me, she has made a separate peace with Time and thinks, as did a certain philosopher I read when young, in my father's library in Rorschach, that "what is, is right." However, as I said before, her minor cerebral ischemic event had clearly brought her over to my way of thinking.

Amina gave small indications of surprise as I began to work on Fidelia's uncompromised left eye. This, although she must have realized by now that I was planning to do further work, for she had already commented, with slight concern, on the amount of anaesthetic I had asked her to administer. Again I was working swiftly and efficiently, as if my decades of experience had all been in preface of this morning's procedure. Still not perfectly sure that Fidelia would not feel, if she knew, some vestigial resistance to my plans, I wanted to make certain my revision of her would be as perfect as attainable, a cause for eventual delight, not shock and distress. I spare you the more esoteric clinical details. My procedures comprised various small incisions, tightenings, liftings, buttressings, injections of filler, in short, nothing you could not glean or deduce from the pages of some of the very magazines that Fidelia, which is not her real name, has written for on countless occasions. Amina interrupted me once, while I was working on Fidelia's left jowl, yes, that vile, vivid noun must be applied, to ask if I was all right and would like to sit down for a moment, would like a glass of water: apparently I looked unwell, my forehead was damp, she said, and I explained that I had never before laboured on a loved one (a "sister-in-law," I had given her to think), implying, of course, that I was nervous, albeit nervousness was not what I felt. *I felt, if anything, elated!* The sculptor is said to discern and exhume a Form dormant in his medium: I was effecting changes that would disinter the face, the long-beloved face, that mortality had sought first to blur and next, at its leisure, to obliterate! My wife did not understand that such a gift could be, that it was possible to appeal and overturn the "kangaroo court" verdict of Time, to find the external and internal facets of one's being re-harmonized, to feel whole again, returned to oneself, and she herself would be elated in time, albeit initially, of course, she would feel slightly unwell after the anaesthetic, and her face would appear, in places, somewhat bruised and red, even if my methods are "of the best," and full recovery is now a matter of days, not weeks or months.

I will not try to describe more of the procedure save to say that a point came, around noon, while I worked on the incipient wattles of my wife's beautiful throat, when my excitement was replaced by a feeling I have never before experienced: a sense of full mastery, gratifying to the ego, of course, and yet indivisibly fused with a selfless access of love. My whole Being, its "selfish" and selfless parts, was integrated in this instant that felt like a sort of culmination, or consummation, professional and personal. I had practised all these years in order to learn what I must learn so as to restore my wife to herself, her self entire.

Fidelia, slumping and only semi-conscious, we helped from the table into the dimly lit, womblike cubicle where heavily anaesthetized patients are left to recover until they are ready to be taken home. I asked Amina, which is not her real name, to leave us and to close the office for the day, and to allow the secretary too to leave early. This notice of a surprise half holiday visibly pleased my pretty young assistant, albeit she gave me, I felt, an oddly scrutinous glance. The cubicle resonated with soft baroque and classical music that played in an hour-long loop. Occasionally I would come in here on my own and sit or lie quietly while ruminating on matters which have no bearing on this account. Albinoni's lachrymose adagio was playing. Soon, of course, Pachelbel's canon would ensue, and then other pacifying standards. Seated on the side of the daybed, I held my wife in my arms, *Pietà*-wise. Finally she opened her eyes, partly opened her eyes, and said, softly, that she felt nauseous, nauseated, I mentally corrected her, and she added:

—My eyes feel tight, Rudi. And my mouth.

Mouf, she pronounced the word, in her grogginess, as the boys had done when they were small. She was in fact quite childlike at this moment, something I have noted often in patients recovering from anaesthesia. I was moved. I said:

—I know, darling.

—Did it go all right, everything?

—Yes, perfectly.

—Feels like I've been asleep for so long.

—It always does. It's like a . . . now what is the term?

—Why's everything so sore?

—A beauty sleep. That is what it was.

—The problems are fixed?

—They are. Rest now, close your eyes again.

—Why does it hurt everywhere, why's it starting to hurt?

I kissed her delicately in the middle of her forehead, her lips would be too tender as yet, albeit they would soon be fine. Everything, I thought, would soon be fine: and, purely in terms of the procedure's aesthetic success, they did turn out perfectly.

—I hope you'll be happier now, Rudi, I know you didn't like what the stroke did.

—But this was for you, darling.

Her smile here was ambiguous, as if pained. Of course, it would be pained. To smile is somewhat painful after such procedures. She said:

—I hope you'll be happy now.

—You've always made me happy.

—And now I'll be like before, won't I?

—You will.

—I'm so sleepy, though.

—Go back to sleep for a while, *mi Schatz*. We'll go home when you're ready.

She stretched her lips: another brave smile.

—More beauty sleep? she asked.

—Exactly.

—I shouldn't look in a mirror yet, I guess?

—Not yet.

—I don't mind.

—No, darling, I said, thinking of her modesty, of how agreeable she had been, about most things in our life: you have never minded.

You're Going to Live

At first we posted guards outside the colonel's cell on rotating shifts, day and night, but for two weeks he meekly followed our instructions, he spoke rationally, he respected the whole staff, may I, excuse me, please and thank you. So we took him off strict suicide watch. Some prisoners try climbing onto the steel sink and diving headfirst, arms at their sides, onto the concrete floor. It rarely works. At the last moment most of them instinctively fend out an arm and break their wrists instead of their heads. Whatever you think you want, your body has a mind of its own and you can't make it want to die.

I'm doing one of my walks down the segregation corridor, looking in on the four occupied cells, when I hear an odd sound from the colonel's cell. I walk back up the range, lift the grilled slat and peer through. I can't make sense of what I see. Under his grey blanket the colonel—it can only be him, though you wouldn't know it from here—is thrashing around and making gulping sounds. For a moment I think he's having a really bad dream, which wouldn't be surprising under the circumstances, except it's noon and he's always wide awake at noon, sitting on his cot with excellent posture, feet on the floor, a book open in his hands, the blanket beside him folded neatly, almost contritely. I pull out my handset and call for help. I'm on my own—Rinaldi is on break and Taylor, last I saw, was charging into the bathroom, his stomach giving him grief all morning.

I'm not supposed to go into a seg cell alone, but backup will arrive in a minute at most and I have a stun gun in my hand. How much can happen in a minute? But now I can't get the key in—somehow something has been forced into the lock. I keep trying while ramming my shoulder into the door, hoping to jar loose whatever's in there.

"Colonel, you all right?" I'm yelling stupidly.

More of those sounds, like he's trying to swallow something and cough it up at the same time.

"Unblock it, sir—let me in!" I feel something give, the key clicks, I haul the door outward. From where I stand tensed on the threshold to where he's writhing on his cot is just a couple of strides. "Need help here now!" I holler back into the corridor.

I'm assuming he wants to hurt him*self* somehow, not me, and I'm younger than he is and way stronger, but I'm scared all the same. He could be faking. Turns out he has spent a lifetime faking stuff and not just in the small ways we all do. Plus it's like there's something non-human under the blanket, moving nonsensically, spastically, making bestial sounds. In different circumstances it might look funny—a kid at a sleepover, wired and giddy, clowning for friends. One of my own kids, clowning.

My hearing is weirdly alert and the rasps and grunts seem more and more amplified. "Throw it off, sir—the blanket." In the distance a toilet flushes. I cross the cell in two steps, clutch the writhing blanket in my fist and, recoiling, pull it clear. He's lying on his side, his pampered, well-fed face purple and mouth gawped open. His brown eyes roll up to meet mine like a veal calf's. I drop to one knee, holster the stun gun, grab my handset and say, "Get a doctor down here."

Down the corridor a door slams, voices yell.

"Have to pull it out," I tell him. My voice is thin, throttled. "Don't move. Try to bite me and I'll break your jaw."

He twists his body away so he is facing the wall—where now I notice lines of words, graffiti in yellow fingerpaint. Then the smell hits me—mustard. His squirming twines the blanket tighter. My eye takes in NO LONGER ABLE TO ENDURE, while an oddly calm quadrant of my brain wonders, *Why not the shortest words possible, with only a few squeeze packets of mustard?* He slams his red, shining forehead against the daubed wall, maybe not as hard as intended—he is weakening as his body fights for air, as his body fights him, the colonel wanting to die, his body insisting on more life, life at any price, life in any form. It's like his body *wants* him to walk into that courtroom tomorrow, wants him to face the judge and the attorneys and the media and the jury and the seething families of those young men. Those boys. MY CULPABILITY, the wall says and I wonder, *Why not just "guilt"?*

95

I tell myself I too want him dead, that it's a shame we don't do that to killers up here—a man in his position, too, a position of trust and prestige, a man respected, revered, imitated. He must have thought he was specially exempt on all levels, maybe all the way up to God. For a long time I guess he was. I mean, who'd have given odds? Not the cops, he must have felt. They weren't smart enough to finger *him*. But they got him, and now if anybody deserved to die he did, and I thought I wanted that too, but I'm not supposed to let it happen and now, it seems, I genuinely don't want it to happen—I'm restraining him the way I've been trained to, pinning him under my torso, my hand forcing his head sideways into the thin, smelly pillow. "Stop!" I keep begging him.

I've immobilized him. Now I have to remove whatever's choking him. The others are almost here, steps pounding in the corridor, but I don't need them. I will do this, do this to the colonel, do it in my own way. He's bucking beneath me. How does a face go this colour? I smell his fear, or maybe my own fear. I hear his muffled, heaving grunts, like there's something alive in his throat trying to come out. If you passed the cell and knew no better, you'd think: prison rape, torture, some kind of brutal, excruciating intimacy. PROFOUND REMORSE AND SHAME. I force fingers into his mouth and I whisper in his ear, "Bite me and I'll kill you." It's completely untrue—nothing he can do now would prompt me to help him die.

I pinch something and tug and it starts to come, a spiral ribbon of sodden paper. He sputters, retches. The rest pulls free: the remains of a cardboard toilet roll stuffed with bits

96

of foil, emptied mustard packets. He's gulping air helplessly. His inflamed eyes stare at the wall and shine with sudden tears. Others crowd into the cell behind us.

"Keep back," I say. "I've got this."

"Oh . . . God," the colonel gets out in a sort of death rattle, though his breathing is slowing to normal, whatever normal is for someone like him. Every second he is more inescapably alive, tears streaming.

His body, of course, could not be more normal.

"You're going to live," I hear myself tell him, to no clear purpose. I hope the others didn't hear. Someone is pulling me off him—not roughly, like I'm an attacker, the victor of a cell fight, but gently, like I'm a mourner leaning over the casket of the brother I always hated, not quite able to tear myself away.

Who
Now Lies
Sleeping

DUNCAN

My son has come home with the ashes of his husband. This is the word he uses, "husband." I've never used it until now and I don't mean to use it again, though the alternatives aren't much better. I know "lover" is the word he used to use—with other people, never with me—a word nobody around here would use about any kind of couple. Not that the word is too graphic, though it is. Such an unpractically romantic and hopeful view of life. Big-city pretension.

They were "married" down in the city this summer, when Jem's friend, Ethan, was already dying of AIDS. I met this Ethan just once, five or six years ago, in the city, when I was still telling myself that he was simply Jem's roommate. Looking back, I see that Jem's mother—my late wife, Meg—had long since given up trying to dupe herself, and frankly, by that point it was a stretch to believe anything but the truth. I hate when those moments come. When Meg died last year—it was pancreatic cancer—Jem did not bring Ethan up to the funeral and I was deeply relieved, even grateful, though I realized Jem was not trying to do me any favours. Ethan was simply too ill to travel.

Which scared the hell out of me, and still does. Jem has assured Terri that he tests negative himself, and since he and Terri have always had such a close and candid rapport, I ought to believe it. I tell myself I believe it. I know he may be trying to spare me. A father's mandate is to die before his son and a son's duty is not to die before his parents. Jem understands the contract. He has survived his mother, at least. If he is trying to protect me, I'm not ungrateful. And if he is lying, he is lying with a calm and dogged dedication, just as he lied—to us—about his life with Ethan, and the ones before Ethan, down there in the city, where nobody, he tells me now, gives a shit anymore who you're involved with. As if I know nothing about the city. As if I can't see that he's patronizing me, the way city people have been doing to folks up here for a century.

Those lies, the ones about Ethan, finally became a formality, elective and consensual, a mutual pantomime so effective that it was still possible, for me, to avoid the truth for twenty-three hours and fifty-five minutes a day. Jem's part in that performance I saw as another act of consideration, further cause to be grateful. And maybe that should have sufficed. But at times I still felt betrayed—not by the lies, you understand, but by the fact behind them. At times, I still feel it. In the three weeks since Ethan's death Jem has grown uncompromising—adamant—and now he comes home with these ashes.

I mean to make a run for mayor next year. I could easily win. If you discount my seven years away at university and law school, I've lived my whole life around here, practised up here for thirty-four years, served on boards, committees, service clubs. The incumbent moved up to the township a mere decade ago and is named, of all things, Keith Richards. Jem tells me that even if people knew the truth (and if I give in to his present request, they'll know) it would make no difference to my campaign. He has been away from here for too long. Suppose for a moment he'd lacked the good sense that God gave pigeons and "came out" during high school. Then he would have learned, if he'd survived the year. He survived because his instincts made him publicly deny what goons on the other hockey teams were yelling at him. His friends, thank God, believed the lie. You could call his adolescent discretion another piece of kindness toward us, and maybe he thinks I should now repay it, but I'll be damned if he is going to bury his friend's ashes in our family plot.

JEM

My father intercepts me at the front door. Though close to seventy, he's still got the physique of a man who was once an athlete and, while he's loosening and spreading, he's not lost his strength or force of presence. His ample paunch is solid, not soft. Wide shoulders, no neck, the granite jaw of a mob enforcer in a noir film.

"Sorry for your loss, son," he says in a formal baritone, as if speaking in public.

"Sorry you couldn't be there," I say.

"The funeral? I thought it was just a few friends."

"And I thought you'd prefer not to come."

Above his colourless eyes—alert, embedded way back in the sockets—the frown lines deepen. The seam where the wrinkled, crepe-like skin of his forehead meets the smooth, red, freckled scalp always stops me; it looks artificial, as though he's an actor wearing a latex cap to play a bald guy.

"You coming in, Jem? It's cold."

There's still no way around him.

"And it wasn't a funeral," I say. "It was a memorial service."

"There wasn't a funeral?"

"Well—no burial." His eyebrows draw together and I hear myself ask, "Do you still call it a funeral if there's no burial?" His courtroom stare could make a nervous babbler out of the most laconic man, which I'm not. I add, "I should know this stuff by now, I've been like a professional mourner the last few years."

"You'll catch cold. Come on."

A jerky false start or two and we grapple in the doorway. It's like the embrace of two men wearing explosive vests.

"You're thin," he says.

"I've brought the ashes," I say, my mouth beside his small purple ear—its cavity, I notice, tweezed clean of hairs. His jaw, shaved pink, smells of bay rum aftershave: a good smell from childhood I'd forgotten. Since taking on a younger girlfriend he's been tending and pruning himself with a new care that I'm relieved to see. Terri has turned him around, cured him of what he'd become: a widower, rumpled and shuffling, refusing on principle to take the antidepressants that his doctor, he said, kept pushing on him.

His face pulls back, turns toward me. He has caught the note of significance in my voice.

"While I'm dressed for it," I say, "let's go see Mum."

She's in the family plot, in the old Methodist cemetery a kilometre up the concession road. There's a spot there saved for me and has been since my birth. In fact, my full name—Jeremy Duncan McPhail—is already engraved on a stone there, with my birthdate followed by a portentous, slightly impatient-looking hyphen and blank space. Family tradition. Four generations buried there. Friends down in the city—even Ethan, who met my parents once—have trouble believing that such places still exist and that some folks continue to live the way my family has, rooted in a township, expecting to die and be buried there with their kin. To my circle, it all sounds impossibly antique, and when they make their glib, ignorant, entirely predictable remarks, I smile unencouragingly and say nothing.

He puts on a shapeless parka and hulking snowmobile boots. I know that he feels the same way I do: the colder it gets, the stronger the urge to visit her grave—even though, so I've heard, the temperature of the earth eight feet down stays the same year-round. It's one of those alleged facts I can never quite believe. Winter earth is winter earth. I'd rather that she, like Ethan, were ashes.

On the walk north between the windbreak cedars, then the stands of dense lilac brush that for two weeks every May turn this prosaic sideroad into the most beautiful walk in the world, I break the silence to explain what I want to do with Ethan's urn. My rehearsed words would be harder to say if we were face to face, not plodding side by side, our eyes on the road, his profile all but hidden in his hood. As I speak, he says nothing, but his breaths come faster—the loose, diffusing clouds becoming dense little jets, tight fists of vapour pushing out at the night.

The brief occasions I've spent standing beside him in front of her grave have been few, but they loom large, and seem long. I never know what to do with myself. I lock my hands in front of my crotch to keep them still. I feel my father's awkwardness too, and wonder if he feels the same way when he's here alone. The one time I came here alone, I talked to her, as if I thought she could hear me. I would ask her now about the ashes, if I could, and if she could, I think she would answer, *Fine, why not?*

His stone, DUNCAN JAMES MACPHAIL, 1939–, is to the right of her stone, mine to the left. Now I notice that the lilac bushes around our plot are as neatly regulated as suburban hedges, while in the rest of the cemetery they've run wild. These headstones, and a dozen more around them—various MacPhails, including my stillborn older brother, David—are all clear of snow, down to their bases, while the other stones receding around them are obscured in the drifts, some totally buried. I wonder how often my father comes up here. This pent, primed silence—maybe a minute's worth by now—makes me want to seize and shake him, shout unthinkable obscenities, run howling among the graves.

I was Meg's best friend for about eight years before she passed. From the outside it must have looked like an odd relationship, me young enough to be her daughter, or nearly, just five years older than Jem. But Meg was always saying how she preferred younger friends—how women her own age seemed prematurely old, cramped into their habits.

Our thing was breeding and showing dogs, Samoyeds. Six years ago we merged my small kennel and her larger one and we attended shows all over the continent, eventually producing three champions. You'd think I'd have been the one running around the ring with the dogs, but Meg always gaited them. I have a bone condition—a kind of spinal arthritis—so any running, thumping up and down, is painful. I took up tai chi four years ago, when a studio opened down in Uxbridge, and in fact Meg joined me at the tai chi soon after, so there was that between us too.

After she passed, I maintained the kennel for a few months but was finding it way too much to manage alone. Duncan never had much interest in it. So in June, when he and I started dating, if that's the word for what we were doing, I sold off the remaining pups and novices and closed the business. I kept one of the males, Samson, and Duncan kept the old dowager, Nadya, Meg's favourite, and nowadays we still walk them together whenever I'm staying up at his house (my apartment is down in the village). As it happens, I was out walking both dogs when Jem arrived home with Ethan's ashes.

As word spread about Duncan and me, some folks naturally wondered if we had been involved when Meg was alive. The answer to that question is no, absolutely not, and not a single person who ever asked me, however coyly and indirectly, ever asked again. Of course, Duncan is anxious that nobody think "affair," not just because it is a lie but because it would make his run for mayor totally impossible. The township is one of those places where most residents, maybe because their roots run so deep, have especially strong ideas about what their neighbours deserve, and why. They also have peculiar ideas about who actually is a neighbour—I've been up here since I was eight, and I'm still just a Toronto girl who moved north.

JEM

We return from the frozen cemetery in silence and have Christmas Eve dinner in silence, or something close to silence, despite Terri's best efforts. All the same, I eat a solid meal for the first time in weeks. My mind no longer regards this place as home, yet it seems that some part of my body still does.

After we finish Terri's pumpkin and sweet potato pie— my mother's old recipe—my father says that he's going out to shovel the snow off the rink, to get it ready for the night's flooding. This is the second winter that he's maintained a small hockey rink behind the house; he's started coaching township kids again. Terri and I are already at the sink dealing with the few dishes. She points out to him that we've had barely a dusting of snow today, and she gives the word "barely" a slightly peeved, weary emphasis that makes her sound years older than she is.

Hunched over, pulling on his snowmobile boots, my father grunts, which may or may not be a response.

"Guess I'll come help," I say, as if there really is work to be done.

"I won't be ten minutes. Don't worry about it."

"I could use the air."

"The flooding won't work," he adds sternly, as if I've contradicted him, "unless the ice is perfectly clear."

We stand on the rink by the low boards—a new touch this year, plywood sheets whitewashed to look like the real thing. This year's rink is bigger, too. I can't imagine how much work this must take. We're spotlit by the powerful floodlight he has mounted above the door of the tool shed, where he stores the hoses, shovels, and spare hockey equipment (some of it my own once), and where, he tells me, the boys are allowed to put on their skates if it's especially cold. "A few girls now too," he adds, his brow contracting as if he's a bit stumped to find himself coaching girls. I know Terri thinks it's good for him in retirement, this return to coaching. I can't help wondering how it is for the kids.

Hands bare, he lights a cigarette with a match, then passes me an implement with a blade of green plastic and an oddly warped shaft.

"This the cutting edge in snow-shovel technology?" I ask.

"Early gift from Terri. It's supposed to save your back." He smiles with his eyes, or maybe he's just squinting against the smoke. "I'll stick with the old one. My back's stronger than yours anyway. You've lost more weight."

"Since when do you smoke again?"

Silence.

"OK, I get it—when I'm stressing you out."

"It's good to have you home, all right? I just worry. We worry."

"Dad, it's like I keep telling you—"

"That's just it. You tell us nothing." Cigarette in his mouth, the tip flaring like a fuse, he's clearing a fan-shaped swath of ice at our feet. This little spree of work banks up no more snow than would fit in the palm of a hand.

"Like it used to say on the posters, Dad. It's not just a gay thing."

His gaze shifts away. "But your friend had it, right?"

"I just wish you'd worry a bit more how I'm feeling—I mean, how I'm *doing* right now. The way you would if my ... if it was a wife dead at thirty-five, not a husband."

He inhales and holds the smoke down. "I'm not comfortable with that term." He exhales. "Forget I said that. You going to help shovel?"

"I didn't come out here to shovel. And 'husband' is the word I use because that's what he was and I want him buried where I'll be buried."

He half turns from me, his face vanishing into the hood, his shovel again scraping clean ice. His hands are big and chafed, a labourer's, though with a delicate gold signet ring cinching his little finger.

"Your mother and I just wanted you to have an easier time."

"Normal, you mean—a normal life."

"What's so terrible about that? A marriage, maybe, and—"

"But this was my marriage!"

"—maybe some kids. Maybe some grandkids."

"Well, Ethan was no fan of . . ." I stop myself, too late. He straightens, then pivots to face me.

"Please don't say anything about you people having kids. It's like . . ."

"What? What's it like, Dad?"

"We don't need to discuss this."

"Do you *know* what it's like? I mean, you love someone this much and—"

"Do *I* know," he cuts in, "what it's like to lose someone I love?"

"That's not what I meant!"

I'm taller than he is and have been for years, but I always seem to forget it until I come back, and even then, at first, I don't see. At first I see him as he appears in my mind's eye, bulking over me. Then, at some point, I find myself looking slightly down at him and a sort of vertigo grips me, as if I'm up on skates for the first time and will fall.

I tell him now that the ice looks good. I ask him if he has to flood it every night.

"What? Oh—of course. Every night. Don't want the kids getting hurt."

The lawyer's fear of lawsuits, I hear myself think.

"Twice a night, if possible. Bedtime, then four or five in the morning."

"Are my last pair of skates in there?"

"You don't still care about your skates."

"I was thinking, maybe tomorrow I'll try them."

"I realize I didn't do a perfect job when you were that age."

"What, 'perfect' as a . . ."

"I mean the coaching."

After a moment I lie, "That's what I meant too."

"I pushed too hard. I think I pushed too hard."

"It wasn't your fault," I say.

He gives me a baffled glance.

"Could we just finish talking about the ashes?" I say.

"How things are going these days—that's what I don't get. Call me a reactionary, call me a redneck, it's like majorities don't matter anymore." Any time in my life I've brought up something awkward he has done this, impersonalizing the issue, the lawyer's old trick of switching topics when he can't win his point.

"If I'm going to be buried in that plot," I say, "he'll have to be there beside me—the same way as—the way we—"

"Christ, *enough!*" He flings down the butt and severs it with the shovel, chipping a gash in his perfect ice. "No more! I know what you people . . ." He breaks off, exhales.

"I am not," I say, "'you people.'"

"You can say that twice."

"You already have. I'm going inside to pack."

"Not tonight—it's too late—there's this snow!"

"There is no fucking snow!"

The whites of his eyes flash briefly in the light. In a hoarse, hollowed voice he says, "It's Christmas Eve, Jem—think of Terri."

"ok," I say. "Fine. But you have to promise me."

"What?"

It's my turn to stare at him in silence.

112

He holds my gaze. He says, "Look, Jem, you're going to have other . . . You might not feel the same way about a lot of things in ten years. But we'll all have this headstone there, forever—this urn in our plot."

"You think in ten years," I taunt him, "anyone will care if two men are buried together?"

He searches my eyes for some purchase. "But Jem . . . you'll live another fifty years, maybe longer! Don't you think?"

"I think you're worried about what the neighbours think now."

"Right, you would—you haven't got real neighbours in the city. You can afford not to care." He draws out another cigarette. His red hands seem surgeon-steady, yet the pack trembles.

Even without a wind it's bitter, and I realize I'm trying not to hunch, to flinch and let on I feel the cold; counterfeiting the rugged constitution I wasn't born with.

"Look," he says, almost pleading, "can we just get this done?"

I nod, ask him for a smoke, and he hands me the near-empty pack.

DUNCAN

It's not easy, to be sure, when you're awake in the small hours, odd term, small hours, they're the biggest, longest hours I know. When your public face is put away, no one else's thoughts to deflect or abet yours, not easy to keep secrets from yourself, in safe deposit, all but forgotten. I can argue a case, I don't look the part, I know what people have always said, at first sight like some broad-back rube, a hog farmer like the old man, "If the guy *had* a neck, it'd be red," etcetera, a misreading I often exploited to set witnesses off their guard, then get hard to work on them. For years, whenever my small-hours mind affirmed something blatant but unacceptable, I could argue it into submission, a professional knack, a necessity, a lawyer opts not to know certain truths about his clients, even case-weathered pros would recoil with disgust if they admitted to themselves that said client really had gone a few roadhouse rye-and-cokes too far that November afternoon before getting behind the wheel, and I got the son of a bitch off, a family of five dead in a compact sedan on a Madawaska back road during a snowstorm, emergency crews unable to get through for hours, client huddled in the cab of his totalled four-by-four sobering up and settling on a tale.

Over the years, I chose not to know plenty. But I knew what was being shouted on the ice that night, one of Jem's final games, the other kids rode him rough at times, verbally, physically, he was smaller and thinner, barely shaving at sixteen, though in good shape and *skilled*, nice skater, pesky forechecker, good for the odd steal and surprise goal, really not a bad winger at all, though I guess he never had loved the game. When he was a child I coached a bit, in fact I coached him from when he was five until he was ten, and I did that mainly, I see now, to keep him playing. Then I got too busy with clients, but Meg and I kept him in the sport, pretending not to see his apathy or even, as he got older, sullen resistance— and in this game I can hear what certain boys on the other team are chanting whenever he gets the puck or gets near it or gets bodychecked and picks himself up, *fag, fag, fag, fag, fucking faggot,* and up in the stands a few rows back of the bench I'm starting to burn up, Meg pretending she can't hear, won't look at me at all, so I try looking at the parents around me—our team's parents separated from theirs by a gap in the stands, a no-go zone, like it's mined and full of razor wire—and *neither* set of parents will give me a glance, they all sit slumped or rigidly upright, frozen the way folks get when some unpleasantness is occurring in public and everyone hopes somehow it will just stop on its own—and I am ready to kill with my big-boned fucking hog farmer hands, starting with the other team's coach. But you contain yourself. When you've built up a position, a profile in the community, you contain yourself.

Four minutes left in the game, Jem's team down three to two, and he's just been cross-checked into the boards from behind, his helmet knocked off. I'm on my feet and yelling before I can stop myself and a few players on the other team are jeering *fag, fag, fag, fag* as Jem slowly gets up with his face crimson and this look in his eyes, hurt, a hunted animal, but angry as well, and I guess the ref finally remembers that he, the officiating adult out there, is not just present for a recreational skate and he penalizes the other team's goon. To my astonishment Jem's coach, on some kind of hunch, or to spite the other team and draw a second penalty, leaves Jem out there for the power play, and Meg, on her feet beside me now, is furious, Jem is never out on the power play and he should be on the bench now recovering. Our centre wins the faceoff and slides the puck back to the point, where our defenceman one-times it, fanning a bit, but the shot bloops through traffic to their goalie, who stops it with his blocker, and there's Jem, Jem crashing the net, not like him at all, and he pounces on the rebound and snaps a guided missile of a shot, his hardest ever, into the top right-hand corner. Our side of the stands erupts, the clock stops at 16:34 of the third, Jem's teammates rush in and mob him. Meg and I are back on our feet, embracing, and—I can't help myself—my eyes are welling, my throat is seized up. As he skates back toward the bench, his teammates following slowly, as if in awe, he looks right up at us, me and Meg standing with our arms around each other, both giving him the thumbs-up, and his *face*... through the cage his eyes and face are shining, the way mine must be, but his expression doesn't read *redemption*, it doesn't shout *See what I did, I told you I'd show the bastards*—no, he is furious, his heart is exploding, his blood has gone acid, and above all he is furious at *me*. He didn't score that goal for me, or even for his mother, or for his coach or his teammates, but to prove how much he hates my guts, how much he hates and despises the game of hockey and always will. Inside me it feels like something is caving, a derelict arena with tons of wet snow on the roof, because I know he hates the sport and I always knew it, he hates being out there and I always knew it, my son is gay and for a year or two in the solitude of 3 a.m. I've known it, the other players are right, the child I love more than my own breath is a fag, a fag, a fag.

TERRI

When he's awake beside me I can always tell, though he lies there on his back the same as always, not moving much, not breathing as deeply as you would think, especially for such a

116

big man, and not snoring. The guy I was married to briefly in my twenties was a twitcher and a thrasher, a cougher, a snorer, a sleep-talker. With Duncan sometimes it's spooky. Lying there with his hands folded neatly over his stomach, he seems embalmed. The only thing different when he's awake like that is he is so much *hotter*—so hot I can feel it coming off him, like a radiator or space heater. We don't sleep pressed together, but still I can feel it. I really pretend to be asleep then. I know he is angry and thinking through some thing or other. At least these days I don't worry it's me. I got over that quickly. He loves me—I'm sure of it—in a way I never thought I'd know; he *cherishes* me. I have a pretty face, so I hear, but I'm too bony, twisted from this condition, and short, three inches shorter now than when I was sixteen. I'm also, so I hear, "eccentric," which I blame on the years I spent with older women friends, like Meg, who had reached the stage where they couldn't be bothered trying to hide or justify their quirks. Everyone is eccentric when you come down to it, some just hide it better from themselves and their neighbours. I learned not to bother hiding it and not to care sooner than most. Also, at some point I figured out that men my age had no more interest in me than I had in them. I found them unformed, unfinished, and I know they found my interests weirdly out of date.

By the time Meg passed, it was almost as if, through our years together, I'd been apprenticing to be her husband's next wife.

Sometimes lately I wake up a long while before dawn and his side of the bed is empty. I know he is outside then, flooding the rink, trying to get it just right. Just something to keep a retired old guy out of trouble, he'll say. If he is here asleep, and my back is keeping me awake, I slip downstairs, to the living room, and sit on the pine floor in the dark with the two dogs, grooming them with Meg's old slicker brush. It doesn't help my back any, but it calms me down. Everyone needs a way. Samson and Nadya sprawl on either side of me, breathing, sleeping the shallow, fidgety sleep of old dogs, and around us the combings collect in tufts and plumes, glowing white on the dark floor.

JEM

A few days before Ethan died (he made me promise never to use the word "passed"), Terri came down to see us in the palliative care unit where they'd moved him in November. I was sitting at his bedside holding what remained of his hand—cold, dry, almost weightless—when his eyes slid slowly toward the door and widened. I didn't bother looking—I figured it was a nurse arriving to check his various tubes and accoutrements. "Terri," he said, in a voice that was still surprisingly firm and full.

She was in the doorway, not approaching, as if she thought she might not be welcome. Then I realized that she was simply stunned, and scared. I doubt she would have known it was Ethan if I hadn't been there beside him. He had always been fleshy in a way he deplored, and wanted to change but never could, lacking the discipline—not that I ever cared about those things.

I got up and hugged her, then drew her to his bedside, where she picked up his hand and then, after a slight hesitation, bent down to kiss his onion-skin forehead. I pulled up a second chair. Terri is tiny and a bit hunchbacked; somebody passing the room might have thought she was a fellow sufferer at an earlier stage. In fact, she is tough, stringy, like an aging marathoner, and if her body looks older than her years, her face, oddly, looks that much younger.

"What a mess, eh?" Ethan said. He had sung baritone in several choirs, and now it seemed that his unfailing voice would be the last thing left of him, hovering over the bed when the rest of him had finished vanishing. "Nice to see you here, Terri."

"Nice to see you again, Ethan."

In my hands now I held her hand as well as Ethan's, and the contrast was appalling. Terri's hand, skinny though it was, seemed to explode with fleshly life.

I asked her what she'd told my father about coming down here.

"Oh...that I was visiting someone who has one of our old puppies—I said it was giving her problems." Terri paused. "But I don't know that I had to lie at all."

"Trust me," I said.

"But I think he *knew*, Jem—knew I was coming here. Maybe he even approves in some way. It's just, he can't come down himself. For a lot of reasons."

"I can imagine."

"Maybe not as much as you think."

"You could have *brought* that dog," Ethan said, having drifted and missed the point, as he was doing more and more often. "They let dogs in here. It's supposed to help with our cure."

"You hate dogs," I said.

"I was *joking*," he said, "about 'our cure.' That was meant to be funny. Can't even do that now. I meant to die like Wilde—one witty remark after another."

I said, "I think he planned them in advance, my love."

"I always was a bad planner."

"No wallpaper in here, anyway."

He showed his teeth, which had yellowed, maybe from the drugs, and seemed long.

"Are you in pain, Ethan?" Terri asked.

"Not so much. Good drugs. If only I'd taken my meds when I was supposed to, eh, Jem?"

He was forgetful, too casual, about the antiretrovirals, at least that was the story we settled on. I think his neglect was really more of a gambit, a brazen game—also a performance, both cocky and indignant. When his cell count was down, he caught a heavy flu that became antibiotic-resistant pneumonia. Things spiralled from there. He never expressed any grievance about the outcome, affably blaming it all on himself—partly, of course, because self-blame was such a dependable attention-getter. He never could get too much attention. He never figured out that he didn't have to bid for mine.

"Is it true it's really warm out there?" I asked Terri, nodding toward the window. I hadn't been outside in two days, but I could see that Monday's snow had melted off the rooftops. Sunlight, blue skies, a sort of remission in the weather.

"It's unseasonal, yes," she said, and it might have been my mother talking.

"Want to go outside, Ethan? A short spin?"

He'd lapsed again and now his huge eyes looked lost and betrayed. He snapped, "Well, if you two want to go for a stroll, just say so!"

"No, with *you*, Ethan . . . I could set up the chair."

His tantrum passed just like that and he agreed, delighted now, keen as a schoolboy. While Terri waited in the hallway, I dealt with his tubes and catheter and got two sweaters and a wool poncho onto him, though he refused the final indignity, as he put it, of a lap blanket.

We wheeled him outdoors. If not for the pallor of the low winter sun, the air's dewy softness might have made anyone think it was May. We pushed him slowly through Edwards Gardens, each of us taking one wheelchair grip. Among the evergreen hedges and the stubble of the flower stalks, a few snapdragons were still blooming in a bed along a south-facing wall. We stopped and I pointed them out to him. He seemed to be staring at them with utter absorption. Then I realized he was asleep.

By the time we got back, a new front was encroaching from the north, a gloomy lid of cloud, and by dinnertime— Terri had long since left to drive back up to my father's house—snowflakes were tapping on the window of the room.

DUNCAN

The black branches of the lilac tree beside his stone, the one I'm always clipping back, start growing, long, scrawny branches twining like briar across the face of the stone. As I watch, knowing what is about to happen but unable to

121

stop it, they form numbers, not ones I can read, imaginary numbers or maybe foreign or ancient, inscribing his death year. I wake up, breathe, and reach for Terri.

JEM

My childhood bedroom is unchanged: the narrow bed, the Maple Leafs curtains, the black-and-white poster of a glammish David Bowie lounging in cowboy gear, in his hand a long-barrelled pistol and beside him a white dog of some kind reared on its hind legs.

At first Ethan asked that I scatter his ashes off Hanlan's Point. In time I convinced him about the family plot, among the lilacs, the place next to my own, downplaying the struggle I knew I could expect, this possibly unwinnable fight.

The urn, I see now, is curiously similar in size, shape, and colour to the trophy on my boyhood desk, the trophy received at the student sports banquet at the end of my last season. Coach Oland awarded it each year to the bravest player. "Most Sportsmanlike" was the official designation, but we all knew it was for a less than brilliant performer who showed guts. And he and my teammates picked me. Considering my mixed feelings about hockey, I was pretty moved to get it. In fact, as old man Oland pushed the trophy into my hands at the head of that packed room, it was all I could do not to break down.

I didn't manage quite as well at the memorial service, when I went up—the last of two dozen speakers, after Ethan's older friends and his bewildered, sedated mother— to make a few remarks. It was in the turns of laughter between my stories that I broke down. One story: When we first opened the café, Ethan's uncle out in California had sent us a gift of three box sets of CDs—Bach, Mozart, Beethoven—thus showing how little he knew his nephew, who had worked through classical music's popular frontlist in his mid-teens, and was by then collecting obscure liturgical composers of the Renaissance and atonal Eastern Europeans of the mid-twentieth century. Not sure whether to re-gift the CDs or donate them to a charity, we left them on our coffee table, and there they sat while we struggled through that first month at the café, hardly ever home.

So there was a break-in. We might have forgotten to lock the door—we were forgetting so much in those days. The thieves, in a hurry, stole only a few things: my new computer, the good turntable but not the excellent speakers, Ethan's black leather trench coat, which he knew I hated because it made him look like a young, less bald Mussolini (here a co-operative flutter of laughter from the crowd), and the Beethoven box set. They chose that one and they left the Bach and the Mozart, as I'd explained to the strapping Nordic policeman who stood in our apartment later that night in his slushy shoes. He had a blond goatee and small, swivelling eyes, and he kept his arms crossed over his flak jacket, as if Ethan and I might try to touch him inappropriately (more laughter here). He said "correct" instead of "yes" or "right," and I started counting and he said it fifteen times. So when did we believe the intrusion occurred? I gave him an approximate hour. Did we have any leads that might help police identify the intruders? Ethan blinked at me and moistened his lips, as a familiar prankish light sparked in his eyes. "Well," he said, "I think we can assume they're Romantics."

As I settle into another pharmaceutical stupor, now in my boyhood bed, the recalled laughter—the grateful outpouring of good feeling from people who very much want to sympathize with you, who simply await your cue—transforms into waves on a gravel shore. (When I finished speaking, they played a few of his favourite Dowland airs, and that, for me, was the hardest part.) As a child in this bed I went through a stage where every night I tried to observe the actual moment when I passed from consciousness into nothingness. Then, for a year or two, I fought every night *not* to cross over. Every night since he died, I take whatever they'll give me to help me across. He cheated on me, lied, sulked, refused to apologize, made me crazy, made me laugh, at last apologized, left me debts and a double mortgage, left me.

Rest you then, rest, sad eyes; melt not in weeping.

In dreams each night he speaks to me and tells me what I should be telling him, as if confused as to which of us is living and which is cold ash.

Wait for me.

Everything Turns Away

About suffering they were never wrong,
The Old Masters: how well they understood
Its human position; how it takes place
While someone else is eating or opening a window
or just walking dully along
—W.H. AUDEN, "MUSÉE DES BEAUX ARTS"

It was not yet summer, it was summer as it should be, hot but not sticky, the grass and new leaves as green as they would go, the verges of lilac along the railway line in exuberant flush. With your wife and fifteen-year-old daughter you drove west into the franchise fringes of town in a small silver car that had rolled off the assembly line near the end of the previous century. You meant to test drive several less-used cars at a dealership overlooking a postcard marina on a Lake Ontario bay.

A salesman named Walter—heavy, bespectacled, delivering his pitches in the laconic monotone of a man who has learned not to get his hopes up—introduced you to the three prospects you and your wife had found online. One was a new-looking black hybrid model that cost about five thousand more than you'd agreed to pay. You'd thought you might be able to bargain, but Walter in his anaesthetized drawl apologized that in this case the price was final. Still, the crimson compact was promising—the paint looked fresh, the odometer reading was modest, and the price was in your range. Walter handed you the key, slapped a magnetic test-drive licence plate into the slot above the rear fender, and off you drove. He sat beside you, raking his hand through an auburn comb-over that the wind kept compromising, while your wife, Lise, and daughter, Emma, sat in the back.

"Lovely day for a drive, isn't it, Nick," drawled Walter. Maybe in some retail circles they still train salesmen to punctuate every utterance with the target customer's name, a gambit that seems almost touchingly antique. Aren't folks these days too savvy for such obvious cons? But also lonelier, needier, so charades of kindness and kinship still trip a gratified response.

Walter went on personalizing his sales script as he directed you along what he called test-drive route numero uno. The route included urban and rural stretches and a drag strip of vacant highway where you could assess a vehicle's acceleration. A rush of boyish delight surprised you as the car lunged forward, sweet-scented air buffeting in through the window. You'd woken too early to that familiar mid-life torpor; you're barely awake and already the day has routed you: lie very still, don't get swept into its current, for now let's call it a draw. Then, like almost everyone else, you get on with it.

You were retracing your route to the dealership via a busy road that ran past the backyards of modest suburban houses from the sixties or seventies, their patios and a few swimming pools visible through the trees. It was on this stretch that you became aware, in spite of Walter's autopilot patter, that Lise and Emma were whispering about something.

One of them tapped you on the shoulder. You heard Lise's voice. "Excuse me"—this more to Walter, who was talking—"I think we should pull over for a second."

"What's going on?" you asked.

"We need to back up. Em thinks something's wrong back there."

"With the car?" asked Walter with a resigned sigh.

"Someone might be hurt."

You pulled over onto the gravel. As you turned to look back, Emma leaned forward, her mouth clamped as if she wished her fixed gaze alone could speak and spare her words. "I saw something the first time we went by, but that was from the other lane. I just saw again, closer. I think a guy is hurt, maybe unconscious."

You started to back up along the shoulder.

"She had to point him out to me," Lise said. "Maybe he was drunk and fell. He's lying on his deck. She says he hasn't moved since the first time we passed."

"I think he might be bleeding."

"She thought he might be wearing a red cap..."

"He's there, Dad!"

You stopped again. For the first time, silence from Walter.

"His face is still upside down. His head's back over the edge."

"Probably sleeping one off," Walter now spoke. "Me, I can't see anything, but I'm due for new specs."

"It's not a red cap," Emma said quietly.

You looked hard but couldn't find the man, though you could see the deck, the patio doors, a white-brick bungalow. From your position the branch of a large tree beside the road was hiding part of the deck.

"Could be drugs, too," Walter said. "He'll probably be OK, though."

"He's not OK," Emma said.

You pulled back onto the road, U-turned, accelerated and veered left on a yellow light as it turned red. Silence in the car—Walter rigid, his arms straight out, his ruddy chapped hands braced on the dashboard. You drove a block west and turned south onto a quiet residential street.

"Here?"

"I think so," Emma said.

You pulled in at the curb in front of a landscaped front yard: groomed flower beds, hedges, a blue spruce symmetrical as an artificial Christmas tree. Beyond it, a white bungalow. Picture window, drapes drawn. The vacant driveway recently paved. As you jumped out, Lise said, "Don't go behind the house yet—knock on the door."

"Why?"

"Could be a drug thing—there might be someone back there."

Walter was staring ahead through the windshield, eyes unblinking.

"Be careful, Dad!"

Her concern was touching, then disturbing as it hit you that she, with her sharp vision, had seen something you all couldn't. You approached the house, legs weightless, anaesthetized; as always in situations of potential emergency you were excited, also worried about the fallen man, also leery of playing the busybody, puncturing a stranger's privacy, maybe pissing off some hostile type whose friend or customer had passed out on the back deck.

You rapped on the solid door. From the other side, a detonation of high-pitched barks and yips. The outburst subsided until you knocked again. You looked back at the car. Lise and Emma—faces side by side—watched you through the open back window. Walter too had now turned his pale, despairing face in your direction. You walked past the garage, rounded the corner and ran along the concrete walk leading to the backyard.

Emerging into the yard, you froze. Ten feet away, a man lay face up on the sunlit pine of the deck, head lolling back over the edge as if craning to look across the yard toward the road. The deck was the height of your chest, so he lay directly in front of you. Grey-green face under streaks and spatters of dried blood. The sealed eyelids flecked as well. On his emaciated torso, lengthwise, a length of polished mahogany. A cane? Emaciated, old or ailing—he has slipped, fallen, smacked his head. Unconscious? No, it's too late. He is gone. You have never seen a body so conclusively vacated.

These impressions occupy just seconds. You are caught inside a coroner's forensic snapshot. No, it's not a finished image, it's a fresh print, still developing, the mahogany cane transforming into the stock of a rifle, no, something shorter, thicker—a shotgun lapsed onto the man's torso. Barrel toward the face. The blood there not from facial wounds but spattered up from below. You can't see the wound, or somehow don't see it, in fact you're already turning away, fleeing toward the car. The passengers gape as you run toward them. You leap in, slam the door, start the car and babble words at them, old man, shotgun, suicide, dead.

As luck would have it, both you and Emma left your phones in the car in the dealership parking lot. Walter says he has always seen these drives as a chance to leave his phone *behind* and get *away* from life—and now he adds softly, hopelessly, as if assuming you'll ignore him, "Best not to speed, Nick...We're almost there...If he passed a while ago, a minute won't matter."

Silence from the back seat. You look in the rear-view mirror: Emma staring fixedly out her window. You reach the dealership a few minutes later. Lise and Emma decide to wait outside while Walter leads you in through the showroom to his open-concept cubicle. It's like the mock-up of an office on a stage: three walls that go halfway to the ceiling, no front wall. He gestures toward his chair, his desk, an office phone. You sit and key in 911. You try to speak calmly, quickly. A burning current crawls under your scalp. The pulse in your jaw is like a second heartbeat. The dispatcher, as if new to the job or too sensitive for it, sounds genuinely shaken. You wonder if you do too. Your friends and even Lise tell you you're skilled at hiding panic, sadness, but maybe you simply numb up and freeze.

"I wonder if I should have stayed with him," you say, feeling queasier as it hits you: by leaving the scene, you may have done something unconscionable. The body is alone, as it must have been for who knows how long before you arrived, and this condition—a kind of exoplanetary solitude—now seems a terrible indignity.

"No," the dispatcher says. "There was a gun there, you had to leave."

She gets you to repeat the address, sends two police cars and an ambulance, then keeps you on the line to get your details—address, telephone number—as well as Walter's. He's leaning on the hatch of a gleaming coal-grey SUV, polishing the lenses of his glasses with a square of toilet paper, as you recite coordinates into the phone.

You hang up and stare at your hand, still gripping the receiver. It looks artificial, or like an uncanny motion-capture version of yours. The veins appear green. Your watch says 12:20. You half see Walter approaching his desk, approaching you, this stranger in his chair. He leans down and—as if gently reminding you of the masculine duty to push on with life's errands in the face of misfortune—murmurs, "Dare I ask, Nick, if you've made a decision about the Camry?"

Two hours later, a cop parked his motorcycle in front of your house. You led him through the house and into the backyard, where you'd been sitting, a little chilled, in the shade, awaiting him, sipping a beer you wanted to guzzle.

The cop was tall, had an action-figure physique, and wore motorcycle boots and aviator shades. He sat across a patio table from you. With a pencil on a yellow foolscap pad he hastily, messily wrote up your accounting of events.

It seemed an oddly informal, unofficial practice, prone to inaccuracies. He sipped strong-smelling coffee out of his stainless steel travel mug. You craved something stiffer than your beer but wondered if you were already flouting some statute by drinking while providing a sworn statement. You tried to describe exactly what you'd seen and done—usually a challenge for a fiction writer, but not in this case, not for you. The event seemed to deny any licence to the part of you that compulsively mines and mutates experience.

After finishing, you added, vapidly, "Such a beautiful day, too."

"They tend to be worse," he said, removing his sunglasses, exposing thoughtful, long-lashed blue eyes. "It's a myth that Christmas is worst."

Maybe, you suggested, the first true summer day feels like a leering Fuck You to someone whose inner world is gripped in winter. The cop inclined his head noncommittally. The ensuing silence—in fact brimming with sound, manic, almost deranged birdsong, cars hurrying past to somewhere—you broke with a question about the man, and a little to your surprise the cop related as much as he knew—not much, but more than enough to implode your initial assumptions. The victim was not old, just in his fifties. He didn't live alone, although he was alone this morning, except for the dog you'd heard barking.

"We're trying to track down his wife. Looks like she went out of town for the weekend."

"So he planned this—waited for her to leave," you said, instantly replacing your first assumptions with new ones.

She was with another man and didn't realize he knew. Or, *There was no other man, but she was leaving him anyway.*

"And he recently retired from the military," the cop said.

"Could he have been over in Afghanistan?" you asked, then added, "No. Probably too old."

Were you making the cop uneasy? Likely he was unused to such dogged curiosity and reflex deduction—the professional habits of fiction writers and investigative journalists, along with private detectives, gossips, conspiracy theorists.

You told the cop how surprised you were that no one had seen or heard a thing. He explained that one neighbour did hear something, around 10 a.m., but figured it was a big firecracker.

"Ten a.m. So he'd been like that for two hours."

"I'm afraid so."

The cop gave you contact details for professionals that any of you might want to consult, he said. Especially the young one. He put on his aviator shades and pushed back from the table. "You should be proud of her. Good eyes. And she chose to speak up."

2

For ten mornings afterward you checked the obituaries on the website of the local newspaper until you found him. You didn't recognize the face in the overexposed black-and-white photo—it looked much fuller and younger than the blood-streaked face you had glimpsed. But other details made you all but certain: the date of death, the code phrase "died suddenly," a reference to retirement from a logistical job in the military. An online check to link the surname to the house address came up positive: a paving company listed his driveway as a recent contract.

You made a note of the memorial service date.

From the beginning you'd felt that if there was a service, and if you found the information in time, you should try to attend. Forming another assumption out of skimpy evidence and ready stereotypes, you'd decided few mourners would be present. A final existential affront. The military, you guessed, might dispatch a small delegation of some kind, but who could say? You meant to enter quietly, sit at the back, then slip away before any next of kin could approach and ask about your connection to the man.

On the morning of the memorial service, you put on a suit and black tie but then, agonizing, changed back into your summer writing gear—cargo shorts and a T-shirt—before deciding last minute you had to go after all. You dressed again and ran out the front door, re-knotting your tie as you jogged the six blocks to the funeral home chapel.

Sitting at the back was the only option. Maybe two hundred people, dozens of them in military dress uniform, packed the room. There were confused or curious-looking children, there were teenagers who seemed genuinely stricken, not simply dragooned into the pews. This was a relief—people had come to mourn the man after all—as was knowing you could come and go anonymously.

The too-thin widow, barely able to walk, was helped up the aisle by bulky men from beyond the city—hands huge, rough and red—in ill-fitting suits and loose-knotted ties. She remained seated and sobbing at the front while other mourners went up and spoke at the lectern. Then a priest with a bald head, boyish face, and irrepressibly sunny demeanour read a eulogy the widow had written. Its content, despite his breezy delivery, made it clear the manner of death was no secret. The man had slid into depression in his late forties and then, developing unspecified ailments and daily pain, was forced to drop the physical outlets that had helped him cope: beer-league baseball, fly-fishing, and, more recently and devotedly, gardening.

Now you recalled the landscaped front yard, the trimmed hedges, the parterred and graded flower beds that—come to think of it—had been sparsely flowered despite the season. Maybe just perennials, the stubborn aftermath of his endeavour.

Peering down at the tightly rolled program batonned in your fist, you're struck again by how the hand seems a stranger's.

From a shelf over the desk you reach down a chunky, important-looking anthology and turn to the poem "Musée des Beaux Arts," the one where W.H. Auden laconically reflects on Pieter Brueghel the Elder's painting *Landscape with the Fall of Icarus:*

> *how everything turns away*
> *Quite leisurely from the disaster; the ploughman may*

Have heard the splash, the forsaken cry,
But for him it was not an important failure; the sun shone
As it had to on the white legs disappearing into the green
Water . . .

In a footnote, the anthologists observe that the figures in Brueghel's composition have failed to notice not only Icarus plunging out of the sky but also "a dead body in the woods." In next to no time you find an online image of the painting, though finding the overlooked corpse is harder. But a few minutes later, using the magnifying tool to search the woods beyond a field that a farmer and his horse are ploughing, you spot him. Only his face shows clearly, inverted, staring upward, white against the dark forest floor. You recoil from the screen; his positioning and pallor graphically recall the face of the man on the deck.

Could Auden have missed the figure? He wrote his poem after examining the painting in the Musées royaux des Beaux-Arts in Brussels. He would have studied it closely. He must have noticed that secondary, nameless casualty but chose to focus on Icarus alone. Adding a stanza about the dead stranger, after all, would have herniated the poem, introducing a distracting sidebar, like cramming a second protagonist into a short story.

But visual art works differently—more or less instantaneously, not in time sequence—and the face in the woods is integral to the painting. Partly, you guess, it's a memento mori, one of those small skulls that Renaissance artists planted in the margins of their works as quiet, pious reminders of mortality. And because of the head's placement on the left side of the canvas, it's a compositional counterweight to Icarus, who's plunging into the sea on the lower right. The balancing works anatomically too. The dead man's face, along with a bit of his dark-clad torso blending into the undergrowth, physically completes Icarus, of whom you see only a pair of white legs.

Each one's unwitnessed fate echoes the other's, yet the hidden victim seems more forlorn. Icarus, after all, is the namesake and protagonist of the painting. Its title directs you to find his submerging form. Nor is it hard to locate; his flesh, unlike the dim face in that Dantean forest, is spotlit by the sun. Above all, he's an illustrious figure—a sort of misbehaving celebrity, a universal metaphor, a byword to the point of cliché.

At the chapel the priest, still failing to funeralize his demeanour, read from Psalm 34: *The Lord is close to the brokenhearted. He rescues those whose spirits are crushed.*

A sense of being unseen, alone and spectral, must be a root sorrow for many of the broken. Yet there's more than one way of not being seen. You can feel insignificant to the point of invisibility or—while living an outwardly successful, publicly visible life—sink under the weight of a pain unapparent to the world.

Maybe Icarus, that golden boy, was a suicide too.

Back at your desk, still in your suit, tie loose, collar open, you studied the program from the service. The photo on the front showed a man in his late twenties or early thirties, lanky, fit in the understated way of people who labour physically but don't frequent gyms. His stance: confident but not cocky. Relaxed grin. He's wearing a white T-shirt half-tucked into faded jeans and, improbably, a red baseball cap, like the one Emma first thought he might have had on. Behind him, a chain-link backstop and beyond that a ball diamond out in the country somewhere. To judge by the light and the freshness of the outfield grass, it's late spring. His apparent age, and the birth year cited below the photo, date it to the late seventies or early eighties.

You set him in motion again (isn't that the point, isn't that what fiction is meant to do, and shouldn't this be fiction?) on the young grass, loping and tossing the ball to friends, fielding grounders with that unruffled grin or wincing into the sun as he tracks a pop fly that somebody, maybe you, why not, you then in your mid-teens like your daughter now, have hit out to him from home plate ... You all return to the bleachers and gather around a Styrofoam ice cooler packed with squat, iodine-brown bottles that he and his friends snap open with their plastic lighters. You barely say a word, shyly thrilled to be present, happily swigging the bitter lager, included or at least humoured by men who are solidly lodged in their adult lives.

A scream splinters the wall between the child's room and the master bedroom, Lise shooting up out of the sheets and slurring, "Em ...? Go to her! Help her!" Beyond the wall more screaming, then breathless, unintelligible gibbering.

You stagger, heart punching, out the door, up the hallway, through the child's slightly open door, reach down to a gasping, humid form in the dark. You stop short of touch for fear of re-terrifying her. You murmur the words we all say in such crises, not always factually. "It's OK . . ."

"No."

"It's all right. I'm here."

"He was there—right there."

"Who?" you ask as if you don't know. "No one's here, love. Just me."

You sit carefully on the edge of the bed. If there were light, your pulse might be visible in your throat like a lizard's.

"Sweetie? It was a bad dream. Should I turn on the lamp?"

"No, I can see. He was at the foot of the bed."

"The man we found."

A retinal flash of that coroner's snapshot.

"No, someone younger. There was no blood."

You cup your hand over her forehead, not feverish but clammy.

"He was scared," she whispers.

"*He* was scared? You mean—"

"He. He didn't say anything."

The pulse in her temple is slowing.

"Oh my *God*"—abruptly she sounds like herself again, returned to her body—"I *hate* these dreams."

"They'll stop, my love. I had them too, till I was about sixteen."

You've told her this often. In fact, you had a few more night terrors at seventeen, eighteen, even older. And maybe

141

they don't so much cease with age as shift over into daytime, subliminal, deniable.

"I got them from you?"

Another fixture of the debriefing ritual.

"Afraid so. Along with all the excellent traits."

"Ha ha."

"Maybe worse than yours. Once my voice changed, I'd bellow. Neighbours would hear. Awkward questions were asked."

"I shut my window when I think it might happen."

"One of them said it was like living next to an abattoir."

Nice. A slaughterhouse reference, tonight of all nights.

You tried to save him, love, and you might have.

"Think you can go back to sleep now?"

"I'll try."

If the dead man had had children, might they, their existence, have saved him? Ostensibly you are your child's life guide and guardian, but at times she protects you, inconspicuously, in the way of a guy wire, keel and ballast, a parking brake on a steep hill.

Months later, trying to set down words and pin down, after your various misconstructions, whatever could be firmly known, you decide to compare your recall of the man's house to the reality. But you can't drive out there. The car you were trying to replace is back in the shop, and an unforeseen shortfall has forced you to put the search for another on hold. You turn to the internet to visit the place virtually.

In that eerily paused, preserved little world the sun is high, the trees in bud but not yet in leaf—that equivocal pre-season in your city when the light, as yet unfiltered by greenery, is glaring yet the winds off the lake remain wintry. A state akin to adulthood, when you seldom entirely, naively inhabit any one mood, good or bad. You click on a link and find a date for the images: mid-April, just over a year before the suicide.

You begin on the main road from which Emma first glimpsed him, but you can't tell which backyard is his. You navigate round to his own street. Again, nothing looks right. You check your notes for his address, then left-click back up the street in blurring little surges.

Finally you recognize the house. The blue spruce looks more familiar by the moment, as does the fieldstone half fence you only now recall, and those terraced garden beds raked and ready for the spring flowers. You think of the farmer and horse in the painting, ploughing human order into the soil. In the foreground of the frame, at the end of the driveway, sits a phalanx of paper yard-waste bags, evenly packed to the top, and behind them a bundle of neatly tied deadfall and branches. Ghost-gliding back down the street, you see that no one else has left anything out for collection. Do the neighbours not bother with their yards, or has the dead man always tidied up and set out his refuse early in the season, ahead of collection day?

Gardening, like farming, is a promissory act. To sow is to project, to cast your faith forward into the next season or the following spring. Stumbling on this evidence of his diligence and care—this generative intention still active just a few hundred days before he blew out his heart—leaves you moved, body motionless, hunched over the screen as if the weight of gravity has tripled. We forget how much energy it takes to move a body across a room, let alone from one end of a life to the other.

Now imagine the Street View vehicle, with its mounted camera, passing along the main road not when it did but some thirteen months later, the beautiful morning of his death. If you and Walter, among hundreds or thousands of others, missed his face amid the branches and shadows of his backyard, then the Street View curators who vet the panoramas for legal reasons might have missed him too. Certainly they'd have missed him. The image would remain online, his face waiting to be realized in the landscape.

Desire
Lines

This shortcut home across the ice had been Niko's idea. His father, of course, would never suggest such a cheat. He'd come here from Greece as a teenager—not much older than Niko was now—and worked seven days a week in an uncle's restaurant as a dishwasher, then pot scrubber, busboy, waiter, floor manager, pinching his pennies until he could start up his landscaping business...Niko could recite the story word for word, deftly imitating his father's thick accent, though a full octave higher because his voice still hadn't changed, seemingly another failing, or at least cause for deep fretting, in his father's mind.

Mostly his father complained about all the hours the boy spent sitting in his room staring at a screen. For several years Niko had competed in a game that challenged players to locate themselves on a world map after navigating randomly generated street-view images that ranged from urban downtowns to roadside stretches of desert or tundra. The competitive ranks Niko had been climbing—

steeply during this pandemic year—were occupied by pseudonymous strangers. Naturally, his parents feared that these ranks included scammers, maybe even sexual predators; Niko argued in vain that phishers and perverts wouldn't waste time on a game not played for money and devoid of sexual content. He had recently graduated to *GeoLoc8r* Master Level II, and Grandmaster was in sight, if distantly. He was a confident player whose avatar, Astrolab, often took to the chat channel to mock novices who boasted of scores achieved, obviously, with no time limit and while dredging the internet for clues. As he and the others observed, such cheaters could click their way up a highway until a giveaway road sign finally appeared and then, with a web search, pin the spot to within a few hundred metres. (Score: close to a perfect 5,000.) There were also those fakers who, turning to a second computer after playing a round, recorded perfect games in a few seconds. The system's gullible algorithm continued to Grandmaster them; legitimate players ignored them completely.

Niko was equally immersed in a map-making app called Cartophile that allowed players to morph existing maps into "infra-active" worlds—fantastical variations on their "source terrain." As he pointed out to his parents, who worried that Cartophile was even more isolating, it too had a social aspect, players sharing their maps and commenting on, at times even entering, the maps of others, though always, he lied, in a friendly, co-operative way.

One of several things he'd loved about the school closures was the greater freedom to log on to these sites and dwell there undisturbed for hours, until, as darkness fell unnoticed outside his northeast-facing window—Niko knew the direction, of course—his screen became an aperture into quantum-deep realities that deleted and outshone all the external ones.

Over the past year his mother, a high school maths teacher, had quit pestering him. She'd gone through her own "period of privacy" at thirteen, he'd heard her say. She now focused on his older sister, with whom, against all odds, she was forming a close bond. So at least one sibling was cancelling the clichés, a teenaged daughter becoming her mother's bestie (faintly he could hear them chatting over coffee in the kitchen after breakfast) while the son consciously, even stubbornly, nailed the role of pallid internet troll. There had been a third child, a brother, the details distant yet distinct in Niko's memory: a Greek Orthodox baptism, the funeral that soon followed. His parents had never taken them back to that church, as if somehow blaming it.

"Mr Kumar said he's the only student to get 100 in Geography ever," he'd recently overheard his mother telling his father.

His father—a man of few words but readily audible when he spoke—said, "He knows the maps and names, but what does he know about the world? Nothing!"

"He's only thirteen!"

"When I was thirteen, I was a man, preparing to come here and build a life."

"It could be worse, Hari. Come on. Violent video games, porn..."

Had the ensuing silence not suggested his father might have *preferred* something worse? Niko had sampled porn, of course—and helplessly responded—but it made him feel isolated, grotesque, like watching his robust larger classmates collide, holler, and celebrate in team sports. While his parents went on discussing him, he re-insulated himself, donning his glasses and headphones and returning to *GeoLoc8r*—a Blitz version where navigation within the image was disabled and you had a mere fifteen seconds to guess your place. Too late. He'd missed his turn. At GeoMaster Level II these lost points were decisive. He rolled his eyes as the image vanished. Those dusty acacia eriolobas, that oxidized red earth that ran in a latitudinal belt around the planet, Australia, Chile, southern Africa...the Kalahari Desert, obviously, likely Namibia, well inland, far from any towns.

He'd also overheard his father worrying that he did not yet shave, that inactivity and isolation were preventing normal maturation. And did scientists not say pollution of the soil and water might be womanizing boys nowadays? *Feminizing,* his mother corrected, adding that she found the notion unlikely. Niko found both notions unlikely but did not have to explain why to his father, since his father never mentioned the fears directly. Instead, he urged Niko to come to the park and kick the ball or use the dumbbells he kept in the basement rec room but rarely lifted himself, as Niko pointed out. In fact, why not play on a football team? Soccer, he meant. The pandemic had granted Niko amnesty from team-joining pressures, though it exposed him to more frequent invitations to join his father in activities. His father had been a serious young soccer midfielder in Greece and, after immigrating—and when not washing dishes, then pots, then bussing tables, etcetera—had joined local leagues and played at a high amateur level.

The latest activity was the Sunday Winter Walk and it was neither invitational nor optional. His father, despite his stolid, manly demeanour, rarely issued firm orders. He was more of a pleader, a guilt-inducer. But it seemed he'd had enough of cajoling. "You will accompany me on a hike every Sunday," he'd said, "or you are not allowed to use the computer on the weekend, for anything."

Their house, an old Victorian place that his father had fixed up on weekends—as if weekends for him really applied— was near the edge of the city. An old railbed, now a paved trail, led north through stunted woods still poisonous almost a century after the closing of a tannery there. The path emerged into a park created long ago by dumping tannery-waste landfill into the river to connect the shore to a small, wooded island. Meadows and ranks of poplars planted to leach out the toxins now spread over what had once been the greens and fairways of a public golf course.

Niko and his father tramped up an icy trail toward the former island, now demoted to the point of a minor peninsula. Nothing looked familiar, though he and his sister had once bicycled here, back when they'd known and liked each other. That morning returned now in a summery slide show detached from any spatial or temporal reference: in fascination they dismount and stand above the epicentre of a kill, a red, ragged circle like a wound on the earth. Judging by the twists of fur gore-glued to the path, a rabbit has been killed, maybe by a hawk or coyote.

Nothing looked familiar, yet geographically he knew this terrain, having more than once transformed it into a Cartophilic "map" featuring a defensible stockade on the island, a moat-like canal separating island from "mainland," and a retractable bridge. In the stockade, houses, workshops, stores, taverns, all with holographic interiors that popped up with a trackpad click. He'd used this map to wage bloody avatar battles with opponents. There was a feeling of delicious urgency, and at times real panic, when an opponent besieged your settlement, especially if they breached the wall and sent in throngs of invaders. One opponent had brilliantly floated a cannon across the moat via an orc-built pontoon bridge.

Tall poplars, flourishing on their diet of heavy metals, lined their path, Niko's father to his left as if driving him in a car, staring ahead as they talked or, mainly, did not talk. They'd been out at least half an hour. It felt much longer. For someone who ran lightly on the soccer field, his father when walking seemed almost awkward, stride choppy, step heavy. Yet he moved fast, making no visible concession to Niko's softness or size, seemingly intent on inflicting a workout.

"You'll become used to these walks, Nik. Already you seem stronger. This is our fifth time?"

He would know exactly how many times, had likely recorded the data somewhere, by hand. Although his office desk and shelves were piled with notebooks full of pencilled entries, mainly in Greek, he'd recently started using spread-sheets for his business. Niko sat beside him to help with the downloads and commands. A warm, harmonious hour, Niko carefully avoiding the worry beads, eyeglasses—Niko took after him in this one way—and an ashtray containing the smoked-to-the-hilt remains of the three cigarettes a day he allowed himself, in seasons of stress. Niko had often snuck in and leafed through the pages. He figured all parents must be foreigners to their kids, but here that remoteness was densely displayed in crabbed passages of alien symbols, struck-through sentences, marginal second thoughts.

"Is harder"—Niko's numbed lips garbled the phrase—"when is this cold."

"Yes, we carry more weight in winter," his father said, accommodating him despite Niko's new parka being all but weightless. "But why not take off your glasses? They are cloudy."

"I can see fine," Niko lied—though after a few minutes he did remove them with mitten-clumsy hands. What a perfect day this would have been for a few hours of SnailPlay *GeoLoc8r*, where you could amass close to a perfect score even without the internet. Every serious player's dream was the 25,000-point game. The current world best: an astounding 24,821. Niko's: 23,169. He was now adept at homing in on locations by the landscape and foliage, the sun's elevation, languages on signs, vehicles on the road and which side they drove on, the look of the toy-figurine people frozen on the wayside. If the landscape around them now were an image onscreen, he would not recognize it from his ride with his sister but would know, to within a hundred-kilometre radius, where in the world they were.

"Will we have to walk back the same way we came?" Niko asked. "I mean, this is going to be way longer than last week. And it'll be dark before long."

The breath clouds billowing before his father's stoic face were like empty speech balloons. He said finally, "We are building our strength, week by week."

"You mean my strength."

"This is a bad thing, strength? Stamina?" *Stamee*na, he mispronounced it. "You know that a soldier, a messenger, walked over the mountains from Athens to Sparta with no rest? It was two days and a night."

"You mean when you were my age and everyone was tougher?"

"You know your geography but not your history. This famous event was twenty-five centuries ago."

Niko produced a few empty speech balloons of his own.

"*Why* are you not interested? History—history really is a map too, but of time, of the centuries." Despite Niko's fatigue and annoyance, he was paying this insight some attention when his father said, "Why don't you draw maps of our walks? From memory. It will be more challenging as we walk farther. Maybe you could even do this on the computer?"

"Where else?" Niko muttered, as if the suggestions were of no interest whatever. "That's how they're done now."

At the join where the landfill met the ancient island, there actually *was* a kind of moat—a slim channel, now ice-covered, presumably left so that some volume of the river's natural flow could pass through. Niko realized he must have based his fantasy moat on a thing unconsciously remembered. A gravel culvert bridge crossed the channel. They walked on along a narrowing path into the island's mixed, high-canopied forest and passed a sign, handwritten in large caps, nailed to an oak tree:

PLEASE!!! STAY ON THE TRAIL TO AVOID
DISTURBING OTHER ANIMALS ☺

His father chuckled—and though Niko knew his father's English was fluent, somehow it still surprised him that he'd instantly unpacked an irony that hinged on one adjective.

They slogged onward to the island's eastern point, where the path ended at a small beach, though a trail of footprints and ski tracks continued onto the ice. His father stopped and squinted across the river toward the new-looking mansions on the far side. "Cheap shit," he mumbled, as if resigned to Niko's indifference on the subject.

A small yacht, mysteriously abandoned, was frozen into the ice mid-channel. Niko saw in it a secure retreat, easily heated, protected, a fortress, a kind of island...Why had other boys his age—except maybe some of his online competitors, but who knew how old they really were?—suddenly outgrown the need to locate hiding places or build secret forts? Lonely thought. He was longing for his warm room, his screen, a snack, bed.

His father lit a cigarette. As he inhaled, his shoulders trembled. For somebody who'd grown up in Greece, he rarely seemed bothered by the cold; today he wore a light bomber jacket, a watch cap, no gloves. Niko shivered too. Beyond them, on the snow-covered ice, that trail of tracks. Niko cleared his throat and said, with little hope, "I know exactly where we are. If we cut back across the ice, we'll be home faster. It'll subtract a kilometre, maybe more."

A last vehement pull and his father tossed down his cigarette and said, surprisingly, almost gently, "It's colder than I thought, Nik. And walking home that way will remind me of childhood."

"In *Greece?*"

"I told you before. We were in the mountains. Every year our small river froze. My friends and I would pretend our shoes were skates and slide on it. We knew skates only from TV. But our ice was never thick, so there was more a risk. Often we fell through." Teeth bright in the weekend-stubbled jaw, he grinned, a rare and thrilling sight. Until now Niko had not registered just how rarely he had seen it these last few months. That grin always disabled, however briefly, a murmuring loop in Niko's inner ear: *He thinks the wrong son lived.*

Where there's a will, there will be a trail—that was the principle of desire lines, the faint paths through woods or across grassy or snowy fields where creatures, diverging from existing routes, have mapped their intentions. On the river the desire line of footprints, paw prints, and ski tracks shadowed the shore of the island before deviating southwest across a wide bay. On the far side of the bay stood a red-brick factory now converted into offices, gyms, spas, expensive lofts. His father had done the landscaping. It marked the edge of the city, their house not far beyond.

His father insisted on going first, which had the effect of deepening the path and making Niko's passage a bit less arduous. Probably he would have preferred to keep pushing the boy, who'd steadily gained weight this last year. Niko had felt helpless in the face of that change, a mere bystander. Yet for all its debility, his body seemed to retain a stubborn will of its own, one that kept defying his father's hopes and nature's hormonal trajectory.

His stated reason for going first was that he was the heavier (here he paused, as if not quite certain of the fact), so if someone were to fall through, it would be he. Even though the ice was thick and people had been on it for weeks, under rivers there were always currents—*"koorents,"* he mispronounced it.

Though this was a shortcut and the vapourless winter air clarified, seemingly magnified, the far shore into proximity, Niko knew it was over a kilometre away. He leaned miserably into the headwind, face and mittened fingers stinging. Out here the polar sweep of the winds across open ice had deepened and drifted the snow—a simple meteorological phenomenon he should have foreseen. As he lugged his feet along, his light but well-lined boots felt steadily heavier. He glared at his father's stooped, determined shoulders, edging ahead despite Niko's scrambling pursuit.

"C'we slow down a bit?" he called, his voice winded and whiny.

The sun was settling toward the causeway where the broad river, under its carapace of ice, flowed into a freshwater sea. His father had not replied but began sliding and dragging his boots through the snow, as if on skis, ploughing an easier path. Then he was speaking in a tone of gruff, coachlike encouragement, but he was facing away and getting farther away, his words mostly gibberish. Or could Niko's headphones actually be damaging his hearing, as his father worried? And had he really just cited the name of that ancient Greek who walked all night over the mountains to Sparta? Niko, of course, had only pretended not to know the legend—at the end of which Pheidippides drops dead. *Shut up, shut up*, he wanted to say, *just please shut up, OK?*

As his father blathered on, the path he was kicking clear began to darken in his wake, snow rapidly greying into slush. Niko felt a fudgy squelching underfoot but wasn't alarmed because his father was hustling on, undeterred. Then—still not slowing or looking back—he jabbed a finger down at the ice and shouted something, maybe urging Niko not to worry, on rivers there were always such spots.

Under Niko the ice buckled, as in an elevator lurching down a few feet, a plane hitting a pocket of turbulence. There was no crack or splash, just a low, localized gulping sound. He was fully immersed in the black river, he was thrashing back up. As he surfaced, the shock, the scalding cold locked up his throat and lungs. He made to scream but barely gasped. His father was barging onward, head lowered as if resolved to get them ashore soon—as if he too now felt chilled and tired. The sun almost directly beyond him.

In sodden green mittens Niko's hands, too numb to grip or pull, rested flat on the shelf of ice at his chest. The edge felt solid. Again he tried to call. His thundering heart filled his throat and choked him further. Above the old factory a tiny-looking Dutch flag flew; his father had said the owner was a fellow immigrant. If this were the visual in a *GeoLoc8r* Blitz game, you would guess the Netherlands during a climate-change cold snap and you would be wrong, earn close to zero points, lose catastrophically.

He tried to chest himself up onto the ice like a seal, but his body was spastic with cold and weakness. That was bodies for you. Again, he tried to yell. Between hyperventilations a throttled cry came. His father, far ahead, couldn't possibly have heard, yet he stopped and turned around. The backlighting sun silhouetted him; his face was shadow, but his tensed posture showed a figure desperately scanning the ice. Niko raised a heavy mitten to wave. Just one hand supporting him, he slipped lower. That motion must have caught his father's eye. Stumbling toward Niko, he called out in his mother tongue, the raw, animal anguish of a man at a baptismal font gripping the son he fears will not survive.

Notes
Toward a
New Theory
of Tears

SEEKING LETHE

A satellite view of Cyprus, the island olive green and cracked copper, its outline the shape of Aladdin's lamp. The Mediterranean is turquoise as absinthe. From this remove, no sign of the island's divisions, though from lower down—the cruising altitude of a Turkish F-16—segments of the Green Line are visible.

Day by day, nuance by nuance, the colours of the seas around Cyprus change as they cool with autumn, although for now—early November—the shallows still look and feel tropical. On the beach beside the abandoned city of Varosha they feel warmest after dark. This evening as usual the beach is empty except for the latest sea turtle hatchlings, a few laggards or adventurers not yet in the water. A few days' perilous swim to the southeast, along the channel of light the rising moon will soon cast, lie the coasts of Israel and Gaza.

By the standards of the region it's early for sleep, but some on the island, mainly the very young and the very old, are already unconscious. Across the island, in a Paphos hotel suite, a trauma therapist with the Canadian Forces is in a sort of chemical coma, having self-administered Apo-Lunaquil (29 × 7.5 mgs) washed down with a triple shot of Finnish vodka. A few days ago this doctor—who tends to the needs of traumatized soldiers airlifted back from Afghanistan for "decompression" on Cyprus before their return to Canada—was suspended for erratic conduct. Should he die, the suspension will look like the deciding factor in his suicide. In fact, he simply could not face another night of re-dreaming one of his patients' PTSD visions—one that seems to have driven the patient to drown himself off that empty beach at Varosha. At any rate, the patient is missing and Dr Simon Boudreau is in a dreamless stupor from which, by his own pre-estimate, he is unlikely to surface. (He'd have taken fifty pills, to make certain, if he'd had them on hand.)

If sleep is designed not just for rest but also as a restorative break from pain—a sanctuary from suffering—it's pitifully ineffective. The doctor's theme, the subject of the book now hibernating in his hard drive, is that human history can be viewed as one long, ever-evolving quest for anaesthesia. *Ultimately all of our activities, from falling in love, to praying in church, to going to war, are actuated by personal suffering and our wish to avoid or transcend it.* Civilization, then, is the epic story not of our striving toward higher consciousness but of our efforts to *escape* it—into sedation, oblivion, the waters of Lethe. Various herbs, mushrooms, wormwood, alcohol, hashish, opiates natural and synthetic,

ketamine, ayahuasca and mescaline, barbiturates, benzodi-
azepines, SSRIs, the endorphins of exercise, the oxytocin of
sex, ad hoc agents such as Lysol, Listerine, Sterno, glue,
lighter fluid, rubbing alcohol and aftershave... *Humanity
has never stopped seeking quick chemical escapes from sadness,
from stress, from insecurity and from pain, which is to say from*
HISTORY, *our own personal history or the larger one around us.*

TEARS FOR MARSHAL NEY

The doctor assumed he would lose consciousness too
quickly and irreversibly to re-dream his patient's dream, or
flashback, which—put briefly and mercifully—involves the
killing of villagers in an olive grove in Kandahar. (Army
sappers were chainsawing the trees to eliminate an alleged
al Qaeda hideout.) As usual, alas, he seems to wake up in
the very midst of the grove, except now abruptly it's an
orchard, apples, pears, his grandparents' cider orchard in the
Richelieu Valley where he spent summers as a boy. He wan-
ders the long corridors of the orchard amid graphic carnage,
yearning for the quietus of a single headshot, like the van-
quished Marshal Ney after Waterloo, spurring his horse
around the field in search of death: *Is there not a single bullet
anywhere for me?* A series of explosions like mortar rounds
and the doctor is awake, his mouth parched, his head sawed
open, the sheets sodden and cold at his groin. The explosions go on: a violent rapping at a door.

He looks at the wristwatch on the nightstand, precisely
propped up and angled in his own ritual manner, like a tiny
alarm clock. Four in the afternoon. The date is nonsensical.

Then it comes to him, who he is, where he is. His eyes are full of tears, his face drenched, as if he has been crying for the last forty hours here in bed. Tears for Grand-papa and Grand-maman and the cider orchard—nowadays a trailer park on the outskirts of St-Valentin—tears for his drowned young patient, tears even for Marshal Ney, whom he briefly *became* in his search for a single euthanizing bullet, tears for the adolescent children and the wife he deserted years ago, tears at his recent suspension and disgrace. *Tears are the clear blood that flows after a breaching of the heart.* He mistrusts that phrase, his own, as too metaphorical, too *lyrical,* although in essence he believes it. It's from a later chapter in À *la recherche du Léthé,* his abandoned study of the human quest for oblivion. *Science does not yet fully understand human tears.* In his view, science spends far too much time analyzing the chemical makeup of the actual secretion, trying to grasp how so many different, seemingly unrelated, triggers can produce the same chemical phenomenon. Science would like to explain the evolutionary advantage of tears, all those different sorts of tears...

The doctor believes that tears of sorrow are roughly equivalent to the blood that flows from damaged tissue—blood that then clots and closes the wound. As for the wound itself: In aging we build around ourselves a protective hull, but even the hardest of these can be breached. A sharp word, a jilting or rejection, pierces the shell from the *outside;* at other times, an impulse flies from within oneself toward another, in sympathy, or pity, or profound admiration, piercing the shell from *inside.* Either way, the protective field is compromised and tears are the blood that ensues, first marking the hole's presence, then cleansing it, clotting it, sealing it. Children cry constantly because they have not yet grown a shell; a man grieving his mother weeps often because his adult carapace has been so shattered that for now he is little more than a child. And now the doctor himself, emerging from chemical coma, defenceless, hauled back onto life's stony shores—he is his own body of evidence.

SO MANY SLEEPERS

Among the fifty-eight messages flickering in his inbox when he comes to, Dr Boudreau—now an afterimage of himself, shuffling in flip-flops and a coffee-stained amber kimono—finds one from a Montreal colleague to whom he has confided his nocturnal difficulties. Boudreau skims the message and clicks on a link: an article published in 2003 in a learned journal focusing on the history of the Middle East.

Boudreau notices a sidebar link, "Settlers in Occupied Territories Cut Down Olive Grove," and clicks on it, a *Guardian Weekly* report on a similar event in 2010—hardline settlers, allegedly in retaliation for something, eradicating a Palestinian olive grove—and along with this item a link to a story about a stand of oil palms in the Congo, hacked down by torchlight to deprive the locals of food, palm wine, and oil to sell, and *this* article was accompanied by no fewer than half a dozen links to "related items," including one from Vietnam and another concerning frontier hero Kit Carson and his US troops clear-cutting three thousand peach trees in Canyon de Chelly in 1864, to shatter the will and the hearts of the Navajo, and Boudreau, now exhausted, can only assume that his colleague hoped this chain of links, this tour of atrocities, might dilute the power of the one atrocity rerunning nightly in his dreams. *You see, Simon... there was nothing unique about it... At least they were mostly trees, not people!*

In early December the doctor—reinstalled in his two-and-a-half in Montreal, pensioned for disability by the DND, and still having access to a couple of scrip-writing colleagues—begins to stockpile tablets for a second attempt. He is practically insane with insomnia, beleaguered by dreams, an internet eidolon who in the deeps of the night might be glimpsed from down on frozen Rue Octave, up in his dark kitchen, face ghoul-lit by the glow of his laptop screen. Except nobody walks past.

In mid-February he tries again to subtract himself from the world, and fails.

Doctor-assisted euthanasia, he reflects, has just been legalized. How can it be so hard for a doctor to figure out how to assist himself?

READING ONESELF TO ONESELF

Seems Boudreau has eradicated all ability to sleep in the wake of his latest self-induced siege of hypnotics. Once again he's conscious and pondering in the small hours, listening to Strauss's *Last Songs* and rereading aloud a passage from À *la recherche du Léthé*.

*No study of our quest for oblivion would be complete with-
out a discussion of the lies we tell ourselves, which, like
drugs, allow us not to know what we wish not to know.
Every person has a staple lie, so has each nation. The lie is
the face, the interface that we pose between ourselves and a
world that we fear to face naked. As for nations, are not
most of their wars fought to uphold the flattering lies they
tell about themselves? An anthem is a lie we sing together,
about ourselves, and to ourselves, like a lullaby.*

A small, soft dog in booties and a Montreal Canadiens
sweater trots past on the icy street below, and what in God's
name is it *doing* out there alone? God, so lonely, these nights,
but Dr Boudreau seems to be unkillable, and not just by Big
Pharma; he has considered defenestrating himself, but the
early March snowdrifts, three storeys down, are colossal
and would buffer any fall.

Somehow he can still derive faint pleasure from the sonic
splendour of this music, even as it soundtracks his pain.
Was the doctor a little in love with his patient? Perhaps—
and had he been born just a decade later, after the collapse
of church power in Quebec, who knows how different his
life might have been? The lie is the face, the interface, we
fight to maintain. *The Church's lies; his own lies.* Oh, probably,
yes, he did love Corporal Trifannis, but not in that sense—
more like a son, the son he once had and more or less
deserted. And perhaps he first began dreaming Trif's dream
not so much to understand it better, and not just out of

professional curiosity, but *to take it fully upon himself,* yes, just so, to relieve his young patient of its unbearable weight. He can see that that's probably the case but is too depressed, hence self-despising, to acknowledge what a profoundly kind act that was—an act whose very existence confirms that this is a world worth living in and for.

Boudreau, unsleeping conscience of a comatose city.

UNSIGNED VALENTINE

Spring! The screen before him glows with a *Le Devoir* follow-up on Elias Trifannis, *soldat canadien de Montréal disparu en Chypre.* Trif is still assumed drowned, and now the Canadian authorities—no doubt much to their relief—are closing the case. The article re-quotes Boudreau himself. After his medical discharge and return from Cyprus last year, he was asked whether his former patient really might have murdered civilians and then committed suicide. To the first part of the question he replied, "Not a chance." To the second, "Why not? We know other personnel are doing so, plenty of them." Beside the text is an army ID photo of a young man, hairline receding, the haunted softness of his large brown eyes countered by an athlete's neck and a heavy jaw showing cocktail-hour shadow.

The doctor opens a new file, meaning to compose a suicide note, but then—agonizing as always over the minutiae of diction and grammar—he gives up, deletes, and passes out with his brow on the keyboard. A spate of lower-case gibberish appears on the screen like an electroencephalographic printout of his garbled last thoughts.

He wakes in a hospital bed, body bristling with tubes and wires. A double room, but he is alone. The life-signs monitor shows medically acceptable numbers. To deduce by the date and time displays on his watch—set on the bedside table, though not in the ritually precise manner he himself would use—some seventy-five hours have passed since he washed down the pills with the apple brandy. His thoughts now leap to his youngest child. His son, a toddler, barely two years old, is back in the locked apartment, alone and forgotten—somehow the paramedics missed him when they came for Boudreau! But wait—how did anyone even know about Boudreau himself? The child could not have called for help! The doctor's mind now unclouds just enough for him to recall that René—the least estranged of his children—is in fact a grown man, married and living in Paris, who has never set foot in the apartment. But *now* it becomes urgently clear that a dog, of all creatures, is locked in there instead! Extraordinary—Boudreau has forgotten that he owns a dog! He dislikes dogs, after all, prefers cats, although come to think of it he doesn't care much for cats either, the stink of their litter, their tails exclamatorily raised above their anuses... All the same, with schizophrenic certainty Boudreau now KNOWS he does in fact own and adore a small dog and that this terrier, in its goose-down booties and Canadiens sweater, is waiting pathetically by his desk, *has been awaiting him for over seventy-five hours!* Its name returns to him—Trif. Its kibble dish is long empty, licked to a mirror shine. The water bowl is empty too and there can be no recourse to the toilet: not only does Boudreau lower the seat (as if this lonesome

171

little courtesy might magically lure another woman, or even a man, into his life) but he also closes the lid.

The doctor *must* save the dog if he can. What a fate, to be locked up, alone, forgotten, terrified! Pity and love swell through him. He knows he must act now, but he's unspeakably weary. He's slipping under again. Footsteps in the corridor jolt him back. Somebody enters. He keeps his eyes closed and breathes audibly. There's a scratching of pen on paper, then footsteps receding. His eyes shoot open. He sits up, morbidly sore, faint, queasy—yet for the first time in months he is not dwelling on his own pain. Squeamishly but efficiently he detaches tubes and wires and the catheter, then teeters to his feet and limps around, searching for his effects. He finds nothing. He'll have to flee in this invalid's smock, flapping open behind, but here, look, a pair of institutional slippers, a bathrobe hooked on the back of the door—the robe he was wearing when he collapsed at his desk.

He gets past the nurses' station, 4:20 a.m., nobody there. He's keeling like a drunk. On his tongue a bitter, bituminous paste. His guts feel stricken as if he has been retching violently, of course, yes, they will have pumped him out. He shuffles on, as if trying to mop the floors with his too-big slippers. His little feet, how his ex-wife detested his dainty little feet! He nods to two orderlies, one sallow and unshaven, one pink and pimpled, who wheel a gurney on which a sheeted body lies. Onward he goes through the sliding main doors, in his ghostly robe, while the Haitian woman at the desk calls, *Arrêtez, monsieur! Monsieur, arrêtez-vous!* He calls back to her, *Do not trouble yourself, madam, I am a doctor!*

172

His apartment is a few blocks from the hospital. A warm night for early May. He would run if he were able. In the tiny park off Rue Octave, the blooms of the crabapple trees are starting to open. A detail returns to him from deep in the past and the kitchen of his doting grandmother, how you can make a delicious jelly from those apples...

His body has reached the building, his brain forgets the entry code. He shuts his eyes and his fingers find the pattern. In the elevator, rocketing up, he grows dizzy and his knees buckle. When the thing stops and opens, he crawls out into the hallway, then onward to his door, barefoot, the slippers somehow lost. *I am coming, little one, ne t'inquiète pas! I will save you.* He has forgotten his door key code. Again his fingers cogitate for him. But wait--how did the paramedics get in without smashing the lock? The concierge, of course—she let them in. The real question is, who called 911 in the first place?

The doctor is baffled and will remain so in the weeks to come. Seeking an object for his growing gratitude, he will investigate the question, but in vain. The paramedics refer him to the hospital, the hospital to the police, the police back to the paramedics. Was it the concierge, who has never once met his gaze? "No, monsieur," she will tell him nervously (still not meeting his gaze—especially not now!), "I knew nothing until the men arrived." Was it someone who called him repeatedly that night and could not get through? René, or Boudreau's happily remarried ex? And what about the doctor himself? Out of the chasm of a drugged coma is it possible that he remembered his Hippocratic oath, or simply realized he was worth saving in the end? Quantum odds, at best. In due course, Dr Boudreau will stop seeking an answer and do what he has never once done in his life: accept a mystery on its own terms. An unsigned valentine from the Void. Somebody rescued him somehow, and he, when he wakened, thought only of saving somebody else.

He opens the door and enters. As if crossing a threshold in the mind, he is once more fully rational. Naturally there is no pet, either to rescue or to find dead. He breaks down and sobs, first with joyous relief, then with a renewed and crushing loneliness.

THE LATE HARVEST OF DR SIMON BOUDREAU

Within a week of his third and last failed suicide attempt, the doctor visits the local animal shelter and adopts a balding, cadaverous Persian cat. This animal, subjected to his obsessive attentions, soon fattens up and re-furs. She curls at his feet in a collegial if somewhat entitled silence while he returns to work on the final section of *Seeking Lethe*. Quite often he writes through tears. But sad as he is—seemingly at a molecular, mitochondrial level—he is no longer suicidal. The Void has issued its verdict. Unlike his young patient, the doctor must live.

His armed forces disability pension lends him a certain modest freedom. His conscience heckles him in this regard. The government is not taking such good care of the several thousand maimed or traumatized soldiers who by now have all returned from the war, or mission, or whatever it was.

*The aftermath of war is like the hangover of a failed love
affair, on a national scale. We look back and recall an initial fever of certainty, then the thrilled, giddy plunge, and
then, when it's over—as we survey the ruins and see through
the lies—we can't imagine what we were thinking.*

Where, in the end, are all the adults?

Boudreau has been reading up on orchards. At night
now he dreams not of that olive grove in Kandahar but of
his long-dead grandparents' orchard in the Richelieu—sun-
steeped, photographic dreams of those phantom fruit trees,
row on row. Which means that those trees are not lost after
all, because whatever exists in the neurons *still exists on the
level of raw matter,* molecular, mitochondrial, an orchard in
the mind and heart.

In June the doctor, gaining strength, begins to venture out
for lengthening strolls. He notices just how many flowering,
fruiting trees—not to mention sprouting greens—flourish
wild here in the metropolis, just blocks from his building. He
conducts a little research. Turns out that there *are* people
who collect urban apples for the local homeless shelters.
But who collects all the other wild food? By July, he is busily
harvesting and delivering to the shelters scads of the touchingly outcast edibles thriving in the parks, in schoolyards, on
domestic lawns, on the flanks and double summit of Mount
Royal. Volunteers at the shelters—mostly women his own
age or pierced and tattooed kids—humour this sunburnt,
bespectacled eccentric as he lugs in bags of saskatoon and

service berries, mulberries, thimbleberries, highbush cranberries, currants, rosehips, a few pears and plums—yes, firm, succulent plums, falling on the lawn of an apartment complex and left to rot!—and certain kinds of rowanberry (beautiful and edible, folks eat them in Estonia, though to the doctor's annoyance the older volunteers warily decline them). The dandelions, mint, wood sorrel, garlic mustard, lamb's quarters, purslane and wild chives he presents as a *fait accompli:* a large plastic bowl of salad dressed with a simple vinaigrette.

Purslane, he pedantically informs the anarchist helpers at an anglophone shelter, was Gandhi's favourite green. ("For real?" says one of them, while another, with a bull ring in his nose, holds the door open for the doctor like a dutiful son.)

In September he's collecting ornamental crabapples—he intends to make jelly, so as to offer the fruit in disguise—when the news breaks. His young patient has been found alive, having survived all this time in the ruins of Varosha, that sprawling necropolis on the east coast of Cyprus. An hour later—after reading every online version of this report he can find, in English, French, and Greek—the doctor writes to his son René for the first time in over a year and asks him, among other things, to put him in touch with his younger son and his daughter, who are both living in Canada somewhere, last time the doctor heard.

Remarkably, the world seems to be refilling with children, his children.

A few days later he receives a terse email from his younger son asking him not to contact him ever again, and also—a mere ten days after submission!—his first rejection for À *la recherche du Léthé*. You have to hand it to the gods. Their timing is as infallible as that of Hollywood filmmakers, who ensure (so the doctor has read somewhere) that precisely 65 percent of the way through a film, just when the hero is transcending his or her trials, some fresh misfortune hurls the outcome into doubt. Of course, in a film this setback is merely a set-up for the hero's eventual, climactic triumph. Real life follows a more random script, if you can call it a script at all.

Dr Boudreau pours himself an ouzo with two ice cubes and sits staring at the screen while the liquor louches like absinthe. After a while he clicks over to the file containing his jilted book and starts reading. A little to his surprise (and even while peering through the bifocals of fresh rejection) he finds himself not wholly horrified. So he continues to dip into the book and read with increasing relief, even pleasure, as if perusing the fine and honest work of a stranger—yes, dense with cruel truths but not devoid of all hope. *To conclude, any person's quest for oblivion is of course doomed to succeed: in death. How much better is the utter* failure *of the quest that occurs when one actually wakes from the coma of quotidian life!* Etcetera. He knows the final lines by heart.

He opens a new document. With painful slowness he begins another letter to his lost son. There is no reason why he should think just now of the baby sea turtles who, every year at this time on Cyprus, begin hatching and scuttling down the beaches to the sea, a curious and affecting spectacle the doctor witnessed last autumn near Paphos. In fact he's not thinking of the turtles at all. Still, as he laboriously keys in words, a lone laggard—the final of many thousands—is flopping into moonlit shallows that instantly transform its awkward crawl into watery flight. It soars outward, the bottom shearing away beneath it, as if in a dream where you've been lumbering over the ground working your arms, trying to lift off, then suddenly you're weightless, airborne, the earth falling away... This last swimmer must be enjoying his own wordless versions of relief, elation, even a sense of nascent mastery, as he finds himself in his element for the first time.

The Stages of
J. Gordon
Whitehead

H arry Houdini was a giant in his field, but failure is more interesting.

Jocelyn Gordon Whitehead, the McGill University dropout whose assault on Houdini led to the magician's death, is intriguing not only because his one scene on history's stage ended in such bizarre folly and scandal, but also because of how he went on to disappear—a feat worthy of Houdini himself. That vanishing act was Whitehead's only known success. Houdini's many biographers say little about him. False leads lure you through various detours to the same dead end. Witnesses and acquaintances are all dead or doddering. If only there were a way to shadow him—like a hard-boiled gumshoe, a keen rookie reporter—through the side curtain of the Princess Theatre and out the fire exit giving onto an alley in downtown Montreal, into the Indian summer mists of an afternoon in 1926. One untraceable source says that he became a minister of some kind in the American South, but that trail has grown over too. Only part of the world is a stage. The rest is the shadow-crammed wings, fanning out for miles and years through all points of the compass, pages of the calendar—the vast, anonymous penumbra where most people's lives elapse.

An ambitious rookie reporter is dispatched to interview the Great Houdini in his dressing room at the Princess Theatre, Friday, October 22, 1926. The reporter's nerves surface in loud, rapid knocking. A squat woman, maybe thirty, yellow skin, brown hair tied back and a pencil behind her ear, briskly opens the door. "Eugene Keeler," the reporter says, deepening his voice. "Montreal *Gazette*." The windowless room, mirror-filled, carpeted, smelling of cigarettes and liniment and talcum powder, is crowded with people, and of course this disappoints Keeler, though he has been warned that Houdini is apt to have others with him and has been known to give several interviews at once.

In his shirt sleeves, collar open, Houdini reclines on his side on an olive sofa, his large head propped on a bolster. A few unopened letters in his right hand. He beckons Keeler to come in, sit down. There's nowhere to sit. In a ladderback chair across from Houdini a young man with clerkish spectacles and hair parted in the middle—a McGill student, Keeler decides—sketches on a pad he has perched along his skinny thigh, this leg crossed high over the other. He's drawing Houdini, obviously, though Keeler can't see the drawing. A second student, also in shirt and tie, sits cross-legged on the carpet beside the artist. Squeezed together on a second sofa by the door are the yellow woman with the pencil, another with a nurse's blue smock and head scarf, and a petite woman with a child's gap-toothed smile, making soft soprano sneezes into a handkerchief—Houdini's wife Bess, Keeler saw her at Houdini's lecture at McGill and on stage for the regular show last night.

The last person, the only other one standing, makes Keeler uneasy from the start. Or so he will recall it in the retelling. The people in the room, including its centrepiece, Houdini, including Keeler himself, are all framed on a modest scale, and then there's him. Another student? His pink face is all jaw and jutting bone, auburn hair receding at the temples, combed straight back from a widow's peak.

Eyes so deep-set they seem goggled with shadow. Huge hands that keep retreating behind his back, then returning to link up tightly in front of his suit trousers, as if trying to arrest further motion. He has the skittish look of someone in formal circumstances—a man in a receiving line, a pallbearer at a graveside—trying not to be taken short in the bladder.

No one is talking. It's as if they're trying not to spoil the artist's concentration, though in fact this silence seems fraught with the aftertones of an urgent talk interrupted. The magician's guests aren't actually glaring at Keeler, but he feels the territorial animus of fans constellated around their star. The young artist won't spare him a glance—wants his model all to himself. Something about the big student— his wriggling, his furtively vexed air—suggests he was the one speaking when Keeler came in and is chafing to resume.

Houdini says to Keeler, "You must be from the paper. I'll be with you shortly." Even lying down and seeming ill, he gives an impression of power and self-command. Without moving his head, either out of fatigue or in deference to the artist, he swings his shale-blue eyes toward the big student to the left of the sofa. "Please go ahead, Mr Whitehead."

"My point, sir," says Whitehead in a tumbling rush, "is that those miracles are far too well documented to be, ah... Why, in the case of the Holy Gospels there are four different accounts, each of them by men of, of noted integrity, and intelligence!"

"I'm not too familiar with the Gospels, of course," Houdini says in a tolerant voice. "But my impression is none of them agree exactly in their particulars. And all were written long after the fact." With no visible manipulation he has removed one of the letters from its envelope—even in private he's a magician—and is dipping his eyes to it like someone trying to read a wristwatch during a conversation.

"Sir, although I'm prepared to accept—"

"Not sir. Just Houdini."

"While I'm prepared to accept that all these mediums are frauds, is it entirely fair to compare spiritism for profit with the—the philanthropic miracles of the Bible?"

Houdini looks up from his letter with a thoughtful frown. "Well, one difference between them we *can* be sure of is that in the case of those ancient claims nobody was around to challenge their veracity and insist they be either repeated or discounted."

"Scientific method," the student on the floor says brightly. Whitehead, glaring at him, is starting to look rattled.

"Repeated? To insist they be repeated—can't you—surely, sir, that would violate the spirit in which they were—they were the loving inspiration of a moment, sir, not some—or rather—"

Houdini says, "We'll never know, of course. Though I dare say if I could return to those times..." He pauses, rising onto an elbow. "And imagine if I could perform for those people! My tricks would be regarded, would be *recorded,* as being miracles, wouldn't they?" He gives his wife a tickled smile. The yellow woman with the pencil is taking notes. Houdini's smile tightens to a grimace and he sinks back down.

"Harry? Is it the foot?"

"Are you all right, sir?" the nurse asks.

"Perfectly fine." His colour suggests otherwise. He places his letters down, square to the edge of the sofa. The top one slips off the neat pile and falls to the carpet. He plucks it up, carefully replaces it, glances up at Keeler with a pressed smile. "And you now. You must have questions for me?"

"I admired your talk at the university very much, Mr Houdini."

"No 'mister,' please. Houdini is fine."

Whitehead is giving Keeler a hurt look and now Keeler places him, one of the questioners after the talk at McGill, the only vocal dissenter. Houdini was giving another of his famed lectures demystifying and reviling the spiritualists, the mediums and their seances. Keeler had seen Whitehead only from behind. He'd stood uncomfortably to pose his question, large hands locked behind him at the small of his back, slicked auburn hair, a bald patch in the early stages showing through. Keeler gauged him as being older, maybe faculty. Keeler was taking other notes during the question and can't remember the man's words, just their awkward, contrary tone.

"If I might ask one more thing," Whitehead says now, a hoarseness in his voice along with the stiff formality and raw impatience. As he speaks, the three women on their sofa tense up, become a statue of the Fates. The soft scratching of the artist's charcoal seems to accelerate.

Houdini rolls his eyes slowly Whitehead's way.

"Sir, it's said that you have superhuman strength."

"Well, today I'm feeling decidedly human!" The Fates laugh on cue and a beat later the sitting students join in. A born performer turns every room into his theatre. Whitehead isn't laughing, though. "And besides," Houdini goes on, "if something can be done by a man, even something extraordinary, it can't really be called *super*human, can it?"

The artist glances up with an admiring smile.

"Extraordinary strength, then," Whitehead says.

"On stage, real strength is needed," Houdini says with a note of pride, again rising onto his elbow. "I believe my forearms, back, and shoulders are unusually strong. You talk of biblical wonders. But even Samson was just a man, after all." He knots his pale brow. "Now what *was* Samson, darling—I mean besides a strongman? A soldier? Mother used to tell us that story. It's not like me to misremember."

Bess flashes him a narrow look. The student on the floor says, "I believe he was a general, sir."

"He was a judge," says Whitehead decisively. "Your stomach muscles are said to be invincible, sir."

"Of course, the Book of Judges! Go ahead now, feel my forearm." Right away the student on the floor leaps up and pads across the carpet while Whitehead takes a step closer. They converge on Houdini, almost concealing him. Whitehead bends stiffly down as if bowing from the waist. Somehow the bending makes him look even larger, a stooped colossus. Both men palpate Houdini's raised, flexed forearm and the shoulder muscles of the same arm. His sleeves are rolled up and though the forearm does not look exceptional, the students seem impressed by what they feel.

"But your stomach, sir," Whitehead says doggedly. The other student returns to his place on the floor, but Whitehead remains at Houdini's side, hunched above him. "Is it true that you can take even the hardest blow to the stomach?"

"I suppose I'm strong enough there," Houdini says. "But today..."

"May I try to strike you there?"

"Harry," Bess says, then buries a cluster of sneezes in her handkerchief.

"It's said you let people test your strength that way."

Houdini looks straight up at Whitehead. With a hint of exasperation he says, "Very well, then." He seems about to add something, but now Whitehead bends further, fist clenching, and pounds Houdini's exposed side and rapidly repeats the action several times—rhythmic pistoning downward blows with the big student's full weight above them.

Each probing impact makes Houdini wince, his mouth gawped open like a choking diner's.

"What are you doing?" the student on the floor cries, jumping up. "You must be crazy!" Together Bess and the secretary yell, "STOP!" Houdini lifts his open hand as if onstage doing a conjuring stunt, and at this imposing signal Whitehead brakes a last punch, straightens up, backs slowly from the sofa with a grave, perplexed expression.

"I was not ready," Houdini whispers. "You should have let me stand."

"You go get the hell out," Bess tells Whitehead in a small, fierce voice. Now on her feet, she seems hardly larger than when sitting. Keeler says disgustedly, "That the sort of stuff they're teaching you at college these days?"

"I'm sorry. Sorry, sir." There's a cornered gleam in Whitehead's deep sockets. He backs away as the glaring nurse advances with quick, clipped steps and kneels beside Houdini. The artist sits paralyzed, pad flat on his lap, charcoal stalled over the page.

"Don't worry, everyone. I'm fine."

"Go on, you, leave!" Bess is pointing at the door. Eyes aimed downward, heavy brow in a vise, Whitehead stumps across the carpet toward Keeler. The top of his lowered head still seems to graze the ceiling. As he nears the door that Keeler has shoved open to speed him along, Keeler pokes a forefinger into his shoulder and says, "Lucky for you you didn't hurt him." Whitehead scowls down with startled blue eyes—pale eyebrows and lashes almost invisible, fusing with the pink, freckled skin—and you can see he's unused to being challenged. Varsity squad. King of the heap. But then it's only a school, and student confidence is an intramural thing, declining with every block from the campus. And Keeler likes to fancy himself a bit of a tough, like the veteran reporters. Still, there's a flutter of fear in his gut.

When Whitehead leaves, the two young men shake their heads helplessly and apologize on behalf of the student body. Not a friend of ours, they announce. Freshmen are all crazy now, they say—though the artist now thinks he might be a sophomore. Arts, he thinks, theology, and Houdini—who met Whitehead yesterday, it emerges, and lent him the book on thaumaturgy that he came today to return—nods yes. He's sitting on the edge of the sofa, buckled over, the nurse on her knees beside him trying to examine his stomach. He keeps waving her off.

"Theology!" Keeler says, scoffing. "The ministry's going to be in good hands with ones like him." Sensing the interview slipping away, he needs to lighten the mood, forge a swift connection in the manly mode, warriors quipping at minor wounds. *Talk about your church militant. Now there was a muscular Christian.* Houdini, trying to sit up straight, jackknifes over with a gutted moan.

"No—fine," he gasps, again waving a hand. The students stand awkwardly at attention. They seem to be awaiting instructions, as if they can't decide which would be more disrespectful, staying and watching the great man squirm in agony or leaving and going home while he does. The artist grips his pad as if holding a hat in his hands. For a moment it's angled toward Keeler and he can see that the drawing is complete.

"Mr Houdini should probably not do an interview just now," the nurse says with a calm voice, a frightened glance, and this time her patient doesn't argue.

A mediocrity who wants to carve his mark on the world has few options. The ancient Greek Erostratus made his mark, as did the killer of John Lennon, though now, thirty years on, it seems a lot of people can't cite the name of Lennon's killer, while Lennon himself remains famous. The case of Erostratus—re-immortalized by Jean-Paul Sartre in *The Wall*—is different. History has him snugly archived as the arsonist who destroyed one of the seven wonders of the ancient world, the temple of Diana at Ephesus, while the name of that temple's creator is lost.

Did Whitehead aspire to that kind of notoriety? Or was he just an earnest kid riled by a worldly elder's indifference to his beliefs? Or a big, dominant guy—somebody used to holding the floor—frustrated by his failure to impose his personality on the scene? An anti-Semite provoked by three terms in a liberal institution where Jews were visible and successful? A gauche innocent unaware of his own strength? An embodiment of the mediocre man's hatred of the marvellous? Whoever he was, Whitehead must have been as surprised as his schoolmates when his attack and its aftermath brought him a huge if fleeting notoriety.

For the first time in many days Houdini is able to forget his broken ankle. The pain in his stomach has eclipsed it. On stage a few hours after the beating, every exertion and contortion worsens his distress, but he fights to disguise it and manages so well that the *Gazette*'s item on that evening's performance describes him as being "in finer form than ever."

Now in the dark with Bess snoring gently at his side, he squirms to find a bearable position. To him it's a cruel paradox that he can escape with relative ease from coffins of steel, or manacles of cast iron, but not from invisible, weightless neural impulses like the ones now tormenting him. So it's true—the only real prison is within. Even his will can do nothing against the pain but conceal it, from Bess. His abdomen to the right of the navel is tender every time he presses it and naturally he can't prevent himself from doing that. He does it with morbid fascination. It's a kind of ghoulish flirtation, in fact. He has never betrayed Bess with another woman, but he has spent his adult life courting, flirting with death, inviting and yet somehow always putting off the actual consummation.

The next day, Sunday, he plays his final shows in Montreal, two matinees. Between shows he collapses on the olive sofa in the dressing room with a damp hand towel over his eyes. Soon after the last curtain call Houdini, Bess, nurse Sophie Rosenblatt, and the secretary, Bess's niece Julia, board the overnight train for Detroit, where the company is scheduled to start a two-week run the next evening. And now Houdini's hero facade, that unbreachably tough emanation of his will, starts to fracture. The pain is excavating ever deeper into his gut; it's no longer possible to hide it. When the train pauses at London, the nurse sends word on to Detroit to have a doctor waiting for them at their hotel.

The train arrives late. Houdini decides the company will head straight to the theatre. By the time the doctor tracks them down there, several more hours have been lost. It's acute appendicitis and the doctor wants an ambulance called. But Houdini, as if to demonstrate the point he made two days earlier—that if a man can do it, it can't be called superhuman (merely another feat by the incredible Houdini)—insists on striding onto the stage, coattails flapping, showman's grin in place. "I won't disappoint them," legend has him saying. "I'll finish this show if it's my last."

Keeler surprises Whitehead at his apartment on Shuter Street the following Sunday. Halloween. He has been searching for him since the story broke late on Monday: HOUDINI HOSPITALIZED IN DETROIT. All week the Canadian and American press have been running reports on Houdini's condition, on his prospects for recovery, on the many rumours concerning his injury. Initially it's rumoured that a student attacked him during or after his lecture at McGill, but a number of witnesses, including Keeler, deny the story. Keeler's eyewitness account of the dressing room assault goes largely unnoticed, however. There are so many competing accounts. Most people continue to find the lecture hall attack more plausible—or more dramatically satisfying. Grace Hospital in Detroit is issuing twice-daily bulletins and by Thursday it seems that Houdini has turned the corner, but on Friday he has a serious relapse. The surgeons diagnose streptococcus peritonitis and rush him back to the operating theatre for a desperate second procedure. By Sun-

192

day afternoon, when Keeler finally catches up to Whitehead, the word is that Houdini has little chance of surviving. (In fact he is already gone, having died earlier that afternoon.)

But Whitehead. Keeler has rung his number repeatedly, gone by his apartment, stalked the campus, even stopped in at the McGill boxing gym, having heard it said—and everybody has been saying it—that the kid who assaulted Houdini was a varsity boxing star. This has turned out to be another false lead. Not that Keeler will be able to convince anyone of that; it's too choice a detail, and history will retain it. Whitehead's professors and classmates know little about him. He sticks to himself. Sits at the front of the class, where his manner is (depending on who's describing him) serious; brooding; combative; quiet. He's said to have knocked down a fellow student at the beginning of term and to have threatened another, but the details are sketchy. Despite his imposing and athletic looks, no real girlfriends. Keeler does interview one Lily McWilliam, a short, rosy field hockey captain in a tan sweater and long tartan skirt, who went out with Whitehead on a few dates. "He was a pretty quiet fellow," she says casually, then stiffens and adds with self-conscious formality, as if giving a eulogy at a funeral: "Some people in our classes considered him rather arrogant, but I believe he was simply shy." The dates didn't amount to much, she says. Informal meetings with another couple at a lunch counter and for a theatrical matinee at the Princess, then one real dinner date at a steakhouse on the Main. Keeler says, "I assume he didn't"—pause—"take any wine with his meal?" She thinks about it for a few seconds and then says, "The odd thing about Gordon is that he did. I don't think he felt right about it, though." Panic widens her eyes. She has remembered that Keeler is a reporter. "I never saw him drunk," she adds quickly. "He was sweet. He didn't much like going to that play, though. It really wasn't working out very well, I felt. It was nothing, really."

The McGill registrar, pending the police investigation and the school's own inquiry, will not release his parents' address to the press. Lily McWilliam thinks he might have mentioned folks out in British Columbia, maybe in the Interior? At Keeler's request, local operators out there turn up numbers for almost a hundred Whiteheads.

On Halloween—though by then it seems pretty certain that Whitehead has skipped town—Keeler tries his apartment once more. He's getting a taste for the work. Detective work, that's what it is. He takes off his hat and knocks crisply, detaching his cocked ear from the door as it's noisily unbolted and jerked open a few inches. Whitehead must have been standing right there. Maybe about to leave. His large Adam's apple, like a burl on a birch, is tightly framed in the opening. There are fresh nicks from shaving. Keeler looks up—he has forgotten how tall Whitehead is—at a sunken, red-rimmed eye and rectangular section of high forehead. He hasn't been sunning himself. This outer hallway is poorly lit and the room behind Whitehead is equally dim.

"What is it?" The voice is higher, thinner now.

"I'm from the paper," Keeler says. "I met you last week. In the dressing room."

"What do you want?"

"May I come in?"

"I can't talk to you. The lawyer says I should—"

"Listen, Whitehead. Gordon—"

"I'm not meant to talk to anyone. How is he?"

"Who—Houdini? Don't you read the papers?"

"You mean he's dead!"

Keeler slips a notepad and pencil from his greatcoat pocket. He sidles closer to the gap in the door. Whitehead is an anxious bouncer peering through the slot of an after-hours club at a police detective.

"So he is dead," Whitehead says. His breath is awful.

"You can give me your side of things, Gordon. Just let's talk."

"The lawyer is...I'm not allowed to speak to anyone under..." The voice breaks with a choked, glottal sound, the bloodied Adam's apple bobs. He's just an overgrown boy.

"Now see here," Keeler says, thinking hard, wedging the toe of his shoe into the gap. "It's like in the Bible right now. There are a lot of different versions of what happened out there and they're all doing the rounds. We've got every version but yours, Gordon. Why don't you tell me why you did it?"

"I don't know."

"You don't *know?*"

"I mean, I don't know if . . . You're sure that he's gone?"

Keeler exhales. "All right, listen. Last bulletin he was still hanging on. But it's touch and go. We'll know more this evening. May I...?" He pushes the toe of his shoe further in.

The door is yanked half-open and Whitehead's giant hand, palm out, fingers splayed, lunges out of the gloom and pulls shy just short of Keeler's nose. "Get back! I won't talk to you! You're a *liar!*" He's grey with rage. In an undershirt and rumpled brown flannels, a glop of bloody soap lather on a belt loop; dumbbells arranged neatly in the corner behind him. "Nobody can give a straight answer down here! It's like the Cities of the Plain!"

"Gordon," Keeler says weakly, inching backwards, "listen to me."

"Nobody is ever listening! The truth is there, but nobody wants to hear! And you all lie. You are all just performers!"

The door slams with a cold pneumatic gust, the bolt cracks home. Keeler stands trembling in the half-lit hallway. From behind the door the thump of a hand striking something hard, then a sound of crazed laughter, or broken-hearted sobs.

Keeler has grown fixated on the late Houdini and his crusade of demystification; he has to learn more about the man's opponent and attacker. His curiosity is sincere and yet also merged with a frank, hard-headed ambition. The full story, if he can ever get it, will make his name.

Keeler too wants to leave his mark.

Houdini has been dead for several months and Whitehead has vanished. Just three days after the death—the doctors in Detroit having concluded that Whitehead's punches were the initiating factor, the American press howling for his extradition, the Montreal police keeping him under watch but hanging fire on an arrest—Houdini's lawyers unexpectedly swoop to Whitehead's rescue. Bess Houdini is the beneficiary of a life insurance policy worth twenty-five thousand dollars in the case of natural death, an act of God, or death by deliberate violence, whether suicide or murder. Twenty-five thousand dollars in 1926: a gratifying sum. Still, the insurers will pay twice that amount—double indemnity—in the case of "death by accident or misadventure." This clause has been good publicity for Houdini, adding to his daredevil reputation, and for the New York Life Insurance Co. as well. Now it will cost the company in an unforeseen way. Bess's lawyers rush up from New York City and obtain notarized statements from the two McGill students who witnessed the assault, and from Whitehead himself, affirming the punches were not thrown with malice aforethought—that Whitehead sought permission first and intended no harm. The two witnesses, urged to consider the widow's needs, willingly sign. And after all, the incident *was* like an onstage demonstration of strength, another death-defying act. An accident.

New York Life agrees to pay double indemnity and the Montreal police department suspends its investigation. Even the American press, moving on to other scandals and sensations, forgets Whitehead. But in Montreal he's notorious. In late November he attempts to return to one of his classes, but the sidewise glances or firm, burrowing glares of his classmates and professors are excruciating. He is mantled with dishonour. So he tells himself, anyway. He thinks of returning to Williams Lake, BC, but learns that in his isolated high-country hometown he's infamous *in absentia*. By telegram his mother begs him, *Stay away for now, please.* (In the curt idiom of the wire he hears her gaspy voice,

197

made stingy by tuberculosis.) *Stay away how long?* he wires back. She is unsure. A while at least. His father, the town's Anglican minister, is unwilling to see him.

He thinks of the mountains, the cool, vapourless air and spaces devoid of habitation, contamination; that elevated wilderness where he felt closer to God. He is not one of those who agonize over God's silences and beg to be addressed. To Whitehead, silence is God's natural attitude, and a sign of His presence. God is *in* that silence, a silence that cannot lie. Whitehead is a young man illiterate in irony. Even his parents—pious town-folk, holdover Victorians unfluent in the new era's breezy irreverence—have sensed something odd. To Whitehead, humour is a decadent complication, a gratuitous libel on Simplicity and Silence. To Whitehead, irony and cynicism are the same. Ironic laughter, to his ears, is the music of Lucifer. And Whitehead is one of God's enforcers.

In Lily there were no deep springs of seriousness and yet (he tells himself) he had fallen in love with her. So often her words would fly at him at an angle and skitter by, like wind-caught sleet passing a streetcar window. Sensing him lost, she had liked to tease him, leaving him still more flustered and bewildered. Leaving him. He had daydreamed of taking her back west as a bride to those ascetic highlands he was always remembering (and revising), but when he told her as much over dinner, she looked astonished and he understood that she had been toying with him, just playing, performing.

He takes the night train south over the border to Plattsburgh. As a bloodshot sun lifts over the layered, fading undulations of the Green Mountains far across Lake Champlain, he disembarks and begins walking, hitching rides when he can get them, southwest into the Adirondacks. In these mountains—about the size of the ones back home, although camouflaged in varied timber—he will make good his escape and withdrawal.

He must remain in the mountains, he believes.

At a resort hotel in Lake Placid he finds work as a busboy. To his colleagues, especially the waiters, he makes a comic figure, a lumbering and solemn colossus—a balding adult earnestly performing a boy's job. The place is frequented by urbane, loquacious New Yorkers, a few of them Jews, and since the pay is piddling and his appetite always large, he is soon reduced to eating their scraps. This he sees as justice and expiation. Then a waiter recognizes his name. Whitehead tries to ignore the scandal this instantly creates, but some of the guests catch wind and they too begin to harass him. It is all he can do not to oblige the obese, foul-mouthed circuit salesman from Albany who asks him to step outside. Next he is challenged by a chatty, womanizing bell captain who has done some boxing at Dartmouth; to the world, Whitehead is still a talented prizefighter, a heavyweight. His lingering sense of honour and his pride in his strength, which he always saw as a correlative of spiritual virtue, force him to accept. Guilt and his growing fear of himself keep him from fighting with commitment. He spends Christmas in a hospital among battered, jovial skiers in casts or full traction, heavy snow spatting against the windows, a zinc flask of contraband rye passing through the festooned ward.

Keeler catches wind of the story in Montreal, but by the time he arrives at the hospital, Whitehead has disappeared. No one knows where. Keeler has heard that one before. He finally tracks his man to a logging camp a few miles north of Saranac Lake, but Whitehead's reputation has beaten Keeler there and rooted him out yet again. "Too damn bad," the French-Canadian foreman tells Keeler in an office hut badly overheated by a barrel stove. The man wears sooted, grey long underwear and gumboots and is oiling a double-barrelled shotgun with lard. "That boy, he was made for the job. He liked being out there alone, eh. Kept to himself in the bunkhouse. Worked his acre like a son of a bitch."

"I'm sure he did," Keeler says, nodding as he takes short-hand notes.

And now the trail goes truly cold. It's February 1927.

In stages Whitehead journeys southwest across state lines down the serpentine escarpment of the Appalachians, doing odd jobs on poor mountain farms to earn a meal or a place in the haymow for a night. As with anyone passing too much time alone in the confines of his thought and outside the walls of human habitation, his eyes have developed a feral look, and the things he says, at the rare moments when speech is unavoidable, surprise even him. In June, near the town of Berlin in south Pennsylvania, a farmer is so disturbed by the silent stranger with his patchy beard and unblinking blue eyes that once Whitehead is bedded down in the stable, the man and his neighbours come with shotguns and lanterns and frogmarch him to the county line—a parade of lights jouncing along the road in the moonless dark, like the rushed procession of a secret funeral.

Days later, somewhere to the south, he is stubbing up a dirt road in mild rain and with cannonades of thunder over the ridge of pines to the west, a swollen creek crashing past him in the other direction, when he spies a small figure kneeling by the road. It seems to be a child, huddled under a coat. A boy. Whitehead's first impulse is to ask him for something to eat, then he realizes, drawing close, that the rusted basin in the dirt by the boy's knees must be an alms bowl. Whitehead has nothing to give. Then he sees that the basin is full of water. The boy's lower legs are bare, his denim trousers torn off at the knees, the dead-white calves strangely withered.

"Hullo! You can stop right here, mister," the boy says brightly. "Just take them old shoes off and let me wash your feet for you."

Whitehead tries to get the boy's face into focus. Flappy yam ears jut out through a shiny helmet of plastered wet red hair.

"On account of it's Sunday. That there's our church." He nods over his shoulder into the woods behind him, where a skeleton framework of cut branches latticed over with pine boughs is niched into the forest almost invisibly, as if by some outlawed sect. It could hold a couple of dozen people at most. There are no benches. "You could stay for the evening service if you liked to. You're welcome."

Whitehead works off the remnants of his patent leather shoes, heels fully eroded on the outer corners, soles worn through at the ball, then unwinds the crusty rags mummifying his feet. Dizzy with sleeplessness and hunger, he teeters as he lifts a raw, soiled foot, the toenails knurled and orange, to set it in the basin. The boy grabs it firmly with both hands and dunks it in the water and swashes it around. The water turns wine-red as caked blood and dried earth wash into it. The rain falling into it too. Kneading, rotating the foot in the water, the boy babbles happily about how good the evening service always is, all that singing and praising and everybody washing everybody else's feet, just like Jesus and the disciples did too... Whitehead takes in little, too entranced by the feeling of caring human touch, something he has not known for so long. The boy is saying, "Now the next one, mister... Mister?" He peers up. Whitehead looks away. "Well, I must have been at them terrible blisters of yours too hard. Talking away and not thinking again. Mama always says that about me. I'll go lighter the next foot." But Whitehead's tears have an impetus of their own.

In September, on Clinch Mountain in Virginia, he comes upon a revival meeting in a steepled canvas marquee large enough for a circus. Sharp memories of Houdini and the dressing room return to him. Drawn by sounds of elation he knows vaguely from home, where circuit evangelists hold meetings at the rodeo grounds a mile from his father's rectory, he joins the crowd wedged in under the canvas and spilling out over the corn fallow by the road. Even those most lost in the joyous antiphony of their responding and praising cede a path to him as he moves with a kind of tranced steadiness toward the rostrum where a burly preacher, bald as a toadstool, strides back and forth on a tight axis, like an accused man in a cell. One hand behind his back, the other raised, he exhorts the assembly. *O righteous, righteous words! He is both the lamb and the shepherd, now hear me, you people, I was alone* (HE WAS ALONE!) *and lost and wandering the treeless plains down below of here when Jesus—which is the one true name also of Almighty God and the Holy Ghost* (ONLY JESUS!)*—He brought this poor stuck sorry sinner back up out of that desert into the bosom of his Love* (BLESSED LOVE!).

Whitehead reaches the front of the crowd. The preacher, still speaking, raking the crowd with his gaze, hooks on Whitehead's face with a startled look and goes silent. Those in the front, close enough to read the preacher's face, fall silent too. The rest follow. The preacher beckons Whitehead forward, then gazes up over the frozen faces and says, "The moment always comes for others to testify. I reckon by this here man's eyes that he's ready." Whitehead's floating, starved consciousness seems to follow a few steps behind his body, which is slowly but firmly climbing onto the rostrum as the preacher steps aside. Cicadas and katydids can now be heard. He stands swaying, squinting out at the crowd. He seems to be squinting through his father's tight eyes—his father, who never would preach to such a congregation—and in the front row he sees, sitting wigwam-style in the dirt with great spherical eyes, himself as a child.

The crowd, looking up, sees a tall, gaunt figure, apparently middle-aged, with hobo clothing and no shoes, a high, bony forehead, thinning hair to the collar, a wispy beard and caved-in, firebrand eyes. Like one of the starved and sunburnt prophets of the Old Testament. When he starts to speak, they hear an accent and a manner unlike those of the suspect neighbour of the rural lowlands, of the debased Southerner of the growing cities, even of the depraved and hated outlander of the Yankee North. "I killed a man," he says in a cracked, parched voice, "in my own country. In the city." Then, with new strength culled from the silent crowd (listening, listening!—all one's life since childhood spent seeking that one moment of unqualified attention, of pure, hearkening silence), he goes on to tell them that he killed the man without meaning to, out of pride, anger, some-thing that seized and used and released him, and left him stained with another man's blood. (Old Satan, someone whispers.) So he had to leave his country—although in truth, he says, even up there in eastern Canada he had been a kind of exile, three thousand miles from the mountains of his home—and travel through the wilds of these very different mountains, making his way south. At times, many times, nobody would help him, and others had judged and harmed him and he had felt sure that even God had turned away from him and had believed perhaps he deserved that worst thing of all, until in the backcountry to the north of here he met a child in the rain. His, Whitehead's, body was starved and feeble and his spirit sullied and broken, but this child, alone by the road, had cleansed and healed him with a touch. Had baptized him. Whitehead's saving miracle. God's power was still at large in the world and it was a love like Christ's forgiving love, not the righteous anger of Judges. "And since that morning," Whitehead hears himself go on, inspired, possessed, helpless to stop, "I've been wandering without nourishment or rest, looking for somebody to hear my story."

In uncustomary silence the people have listened, but now finally they pour out their dammed-up singing and praise: "I Want to Dwell in That Rock." The story has the simplicity and brevity of a parable, but most of all it is Whitehead's soft, awkward, chastened delivery that has gained their hearts. The charismatic revivalists who visit them conduct them to joy, even ecstasy, but they are also starting to rouse suspicion. In the last two years some have been caught out in fornication, in the embezzlement of offerings, the sundry deceptions of "healing" associates planted in the crowd, imbibing diluted strychnine, handling venomless snakes or crawdads dyed yellow, their tails whittled to scorpion stingers. Whitehead, to this crowd, seems a holy fool, a man too simple to lie or resort to elaborate performance— after all, he has admitted to the sin of taking a life (which also lends him a sort of Old Testament virility)—and now they perceive how a part of their collective soul has long been craving such testimony.

Word of Whitehead spreads. With the preacher, Brother Virnal Simms, he travels the region testifying in marquees and chapels and county halls and brush arbours, his story gathering detail and power with repetition. Now he tells of how a woman in the city turned away from his affections, of how a prizefighter attacked him in the Adirondacks, of how a lynch mob of Dutchmen bound his hands and marched him away by lantern light, and of other trials as well. Yet the tone of the tale remains simple, direct. Everywhere Whitehead is offered food and shelter and clothing, but he eats sparingly and, although he accepts newly homespun wool trousers and a simple shirt and frock coat, he chooses to remain bare-shod in the deepening chill. To him this is spiritual discipline. It suits Brother Virnal fine as well. His barefoot boy has become an attraction; the liberality of recent offerings puts salve to Simms's mild sense of injury as he becomes aware that crowds are often impatient with his own theatrical preaching and eager for Whitehead to begin. And after Whitehead recites his story, people approach the rostrum or stage and ask that he, not the famous Brother Virnal, lay his hand on their brows or touch their afflicted parts. Word is that Whitehead's touch is strongly efficacious. Whitehead, or Brother Jos (Simms now bills him thusly and the name adheres), believes it himself, having seen the jubilant faces and sudden lightness in the limbs of the infirm, having twice handled a canebrake rattler without harm, having plucked a live coal from a chapel stove with no pain in his fingers and only the faintest pink stigma left after.

In November, near Asheville, he falls out with Brother Virnal, whom he has come more and more to dislike. Dislike, not detest, for it seems the vast aquifer of rage that has long bubbled and sometimes spewed from Whitehead has been tapped off, or dried up. Dislike, nonetheless, because Simms is another performer and a hypocrite besides, offering with a carnival barker's wink to procure women for Whitehead after the camp meetings, urging bootleg bourbon and rye (he can't bear to get drunk alone) on a man who has sworn off drink.

Despite all the evidence, Simms can't seem to credit Whitehead's sincerity.

Whitehead finally breaks with him as they pass through a deep, windless valley of quiet farms, the roadside ochre and golden with butternut leaves and downed pears and apples, where, Brother Virnal casually confides, he once led a prayer meeting right after a thief got lynched. Caught pilfering from a corncrib, and the Black bastard hit the farmer when he got nabbed. Laid him flat out. All but got across the state line. That meeting was like the Thanksgiving after. Kept him in the barn and marched him out to his reckoning first thing that morning.

Brother Virnal's tone carries no special contempt for the thief and no bloodlusty delight in his lynching and mutilation (about which he is a granary of detail)—as if he were speaking of some minor, natural process in God's greater scheme: an animal, true to its nature, caught raiding the burrow of a larger beast, which, true to its own nature, impersonally destroys it. Yet Brother Virnal had preached the Gospel within sight of that swaying, spattered corpse; like a Roman guard presuming to lecture about love on Golgotha.

Winter pushes Brother Jos and his entourage south out of the mountains. The entourage is chiefly composed of poor, rootless men and women who are believers either in Brother Jos or in the potential for some future profit or advantage. Or all these things. Everywhere the growing band is welcomed and hailed. In March 1928, at a big revival meeting in Wetumpka, Alabama, Brother Jos refuses to be interviewed by a reporter from Montgomery, but the story of the meeting runs and is picked up by several larger Southern papers. POPULAR HEALER REPUTED TO HAVE RAISED THE DEAD. Word reaches Eugene Keeler in Montreal.

Keeler, like Houdini—the subject of his first big story and now the object of his emulation—has found his métier as a professional "debunker." A new word for a new occupation for a new era. And Keeler is its man. Over the past year and a half he has written various investigative stories on local quacks and hoaxsters and a popular "Gypsy" medium, Madame Hetepheres, in Toronto. The stories have brought him attention, respect, and a sizable raise. Now, working on a hunch, he persuades his editors to send him south to cover a new story. There's a gambler's chance that the charismatic healer—reportedly large, solemn, and banished in the recent past from somewhere up north, maybe Canada—is the man Keeler has all but given up hope of finding. His hunch is indefensible, yet nagging. And even if it's not young Whitehead, Keeler wants the story.

He catches up to Whitehead on the first morning of a three-day camp meeting on the outskirts of Egypt, Mississippi, during a heat wave in mid-April. That first morning he plans to stick near the back of the mob, but he has to push in closer, into the welcome shade of the marquee, to be sure if the last of the speakers is really Whitehead. It is, he finally decides, hoping that Whitehead—whose train-tunnel eyes range over the now-silent hundreds leaning forward en masse as if on a steep incline, ears cocked, mouths ajar—has not recognized him in the new moustache he's growing. In fact, seeing his quarry so changed, Keeler feels invisible himself, as if decades must have passed and now they're both different men.

Nothing he has read in the past weeks has prepared him for what ensues. The unrestrained singing, praying, and speaking in tongues, the laying on of hands: A gristly old woman with a goitre bloating from her chicken neck like a second chin stands before Whitehead, who sets his right hand on the swelling and prays under his breath. The old woman, head thrown back as if offering the deformity to be kissed, starts keening shrilly and when her voice breaks and she sobs, weeps, and turns to rejoin the chanting crowd, the goitre does seem smaller, though Keeler feels it must be from her straighter posture. Still, the performance, the full performance, is impressive. "Brother Jos" has pocketed the lot of them. Around Keeler the incandescent faces, wrinkles rilled with sweat, eyes lolling back, bodies convulsed—all seem caught in a prolonged orgasmic frenzy, the crowd now a single moaning and many-limbed creature. Only Keeler, like a time-machine historian taking notes at a Roman orgy, stands apart. Starting to percolate plans, he returns to the airless kiln of his hotel room.

Early on the third and last day of the meeting, a corpse arrives at the station in Egypt on the 7:20 from Tupelo. Eugene Keeler, in bow tie and dark vested suit, is there to meet it. Two groggy young men in overalls wait with him. Keeler has missed the whole second day of the meeting, spending it on and off local trains and in towns between Egypt and Tupelo. Finally, at the Tupelo County Hospital morgue, he found his body. A prisoner—a migrant farm-hand from somewhere down in Georgia, taken in fornication with a local girl—he'd died two days before, trying to escape the county jail. Accident, involving a high flight of concrete stairs. They were waiting for the coroner to get over a bad siege of influenza and examine him. Keeler received the impression that no one, including the coroner, was eager for this autopsy to occur. He made a modest offer to the man's assistants, trusting he could wire back to Montreal for more money if it was required. It was not. And no one asked any questions. As the orderly curtained the sheet back over a white face livid with contusions, Keeler the debunker sensed that here too was a story, another kind of fraud to expose. But he was just one writer and it was Whitehead who possessed him.

On the station platform in Egypt, Keeler takes delivery from the same orderly and tips the man, who seems stunned, even frightened, by this gesture. He will pitch the coins out the train window on his way back to Tupelo. So Keeler sus-pects. Everywhere this reign of superstition and credulity. He helps his hired men—two brothers he found idling yester-day outside the barber's—load the deal casket onto a flatbed cart beside the spades. In lack of the mule they promised to get, each brother uncomplainingly fits a yoke-arm under his own arm and hauls. These brothers, Harman and Irwin, have a sort of hopping tiptoe gait, making the casket joggle on the flatbed and creep steadily toward the back edge. Keeler walks close behind, making adjustments to the casket and also to his plans. When the body is presented, will Whitehead, entrapped, throw up his hands in defeat, or will he actually attempt to resurrect it? Keeler preens himself on his unfoolable eye, but he's frankly unsure if Whitehead is a conscious fraud or a mad believer. He feels no qualms over what's about to occur. It would have happened soon anyway. This way, when it does, Keeler will be there with his notepad and Pocket Folding Camera, and the crowd, then the world, will learn who Brother Jos truly is, and what he isn't.

Keeler's odd procession judders along the road toward the fairground as the morning's scented coolness evaporates with the dew on wayside brambles and downed magnolia petals. By the river, new leafage is drooping already, like the arboreal mosses and vines and weeping willow boughs, everything languid, lapsing earthward in the heat. Keeler's wet underclothes cling to him. Partly it's nerves. He wonders how long the body will last. He has told the incurious, drowsy brothers that he simply hopes to ask Brother Jos to pray at the graveside of his cousin.

During the wild frontward surge after Whitehead's story, they hoist the casket, the brothers shouldering the sides, Keeler struggling at the foot, and move out of the pines at the edge of the field toward the far rostrum and the healer. As they enter the crowd, it slowly opens and the casket bobs forward like a lifeboat over a swaying, abruptly soundless lake of faces. One by one, silent strangers join them, dipping their shoulders under the casket and falling into step, so that ten men set it down together on the rostrum's edge at the bare, clean feet of Brother Jos.

Keeler removes his hat and holds it, the brothers hastily following suit. Whitehead stares down at the casket with an intense though indeterminate expression.

Keeler says, "Forgive us for intruding on your meeting, sir."

"I'm Brother Jos," Whitehead says with an incipient Southern twang. "You're welcome here."

"Thank you," says Keeler, the shakiness in his voice unfeigned. He goes on, louder, "I've been made to feel very welcome down here by everyone, and it's been a comfort. My wife and I travelled down here last month to be with my cousin, Will, in hospital, up in Tupelo. His wife passed away two years ago, he needed someone to help with the children. But yesterday, I'm afraid..." Keeler's heart is thudding in his throat. He lets his head droop and uses the brim of his held hat to cover his eyes. "You'll have to forgive me."

"Of course."

After some moments he straightens up, sets his hat down by the casket with a firmer hand. "Sir? I was hoping that..."

"Just Brother Jos," Whitehead says softly. "Where do you come from?"

"Why, from Canada."

Whitehead's mouth falls open slightly, but he doesn't speak.

Keeler scents blood.

212

"Brother Jos"—he forces out the stage name—"even up in Canada we've heard it said that you can restore vital faculties to people—their lost sight, their hearing, their speech. Even, many have said, their lives." Keeler grips the casket lid and wrenches it off and brings it down onto the rostrum. It gives an accusing thud, a judge's mallet marking a verdict. The rustling crowd keeps edging closer. Keeler feels the two brothers' eyes on his hot face.

Whitehead looks down at the sheeted body with frozen foreboding, like a man about to identify a victim.

"Restore this man to the world and to his children, Brother Jos, I beg you."

Nothing. Whitehead's eyes seem glassy with defeat. Already it's over. Almost *too* soon. And yet, now he is dropping to one knee beside the casket, fumbling in to uncurtain the face, to cup his hand over the dead man's shattered forehead. He mumbles, praying inaudibly, for a minute or so. Maybe longer. And then, slowly, he looks up at Keeler, who's still standing on the ground, so their faces are level. Recognition wells into Whitehead's eyes. Keeler pulls out his Pocket Folding Camera and squeezes a few shots at close range, then climbs unhurriedly onto the rostrum and turns to the silenced crowd. Still on one knee, Whitehead has stopped praying. Keeler announces that the young man before them cannot resurrect a cadaver or heal the dying any more than you or I could. Brother Jos, he goes on, is a college dropout from Canada and his real name is Jocelyn Gordon Whitehead—that's right, the very same Whitehead whose unprovoked and unpunished assault sent the Great

Houdini to his grave—Houdini, the magician whose avocation was exposing fake spiritualists and other charlatans!

A hostile murmuring ripples through the crowd. One of the brothers shouts something in a hoarse, affronted voice. Keeler raises his hat for quiet—he wants to explain who he is and why he has come—but the tumult is spreading. *You liar,* he hears. *Dirty Yankee!* Everywhere, fingers are pointing, but not at the disgraced Whitehead. As the crowd's frontmost ranks flow up onto the stage like flood waters over a levee, Keeler gets a flashbulb glimpse of how he has miscalculated, hasn't prepared properly, doesn't know these people at all. In matters of the heart the outsider is always wrong. The brothers and the volunteer pallbearers surround him. Hands grope at him. Fists bestow eager, inaugural jabs. Keeler has broken his hero's own rule: never be impatient. The last thing he sees is Whitehead—eyes fastened on him with revived hurt, anger, even loathing—shoving in to save him from the mob.

In the stifling woodshed among the pines, Brother Jos huddles over Keeler and prays. His right hand is clamped over the man's wet, scalding brow. A doctor has been sent for in Tupelo, but Brother Jos is striving to heal the damaged body now, through silent prayer and touch—to help Keeler to his feet and safely away. He can't even bring the man to, or settle his fever. The power, the Charisma that Brother Jos has felt growing in himself over the last year is leaking steadily out of him like blood from a neat, efficient puncture.

Keeler's blood. Eugene Keeler is going to live to tell his story, but Brother Jos—J. Gordon Whitehead—knows himself to be finished.

He might have resisted the lure of suicide among those sturdy, serviceable pines and, disgraced in his own mind, wandered off again, southwest over the corn and cotton flatlands of Mississippi and Louisiana, then the treeless Texas plains, feeling exposed, cut through by the sun's adjudicating eye, its light probing to the void core of him. Indifferently he pushed on, always westward, toward the Rockies. Maybe in Albuquerque he enlisted as a hand with a China-bound Methodist missionary, not so much to further the work of the Church as to go elsewhere, anywhere.

Somehow or other he died far away. It might have happened early on, Whitehead ignoring a crewman's warning to lie flat on the deck of a barge chugging up through one of the Yangtze gorges while bullets flitted overhead with a sound like someone tearing pages out of a book. Or he might have pushed on to the west in search of higher, deeper mountains, the traditional enclaves of the failed and the shamed, spurred on by rumours of a land on the far side of the Himalayas where people were still innocents, whose uncorrupted tongue could not shape itself to sarcasm or irony.

By and large the Nepali tongue is still like that. In the fall of 1988 I was in the Kingdom of Nepal for some time, trekking and learning the language from a chatty primer printed on rank, hairy paper. The book's sweet-natured author entreated students never to use irony when addressing a Nepali. They would not understand. They would take what you said literally. I was touched by the notion that this mountain fastness had not been infiltrated by the temper of the times, with its ironies layered on ironies, though as part of a small but growing occupying force of Western tourists I had to admit, with a sense of complicity, that it was likely just a matter of when. I couldn't have stayed. I didn't belong to that alien place, and time; though some people always will love most what they least belong to.

But Whitehead. He might have belonged, might have stayed, for fifty, sixty years. Not impossibly he was the very large old man I encountered on the trail up Mount Nagar-jun, on the outskirts of Kathmandu, in November '88. I was climbing into a slow, fluttering rain of pastel-tinted tissue squares, imprinted with verses of Buddhist scripture, flung into space off the summit visible two hours' hike above. Up there, at intervals, tiny silhouettes would exert themselves and there would be another pink, white, blue, or lavender eruption, then the gradual, gorgeous dissemination of prayer sheets on the wind. They were charting the wind's convoluted patterns the way plum blossoms on a river show currents. I picked up a few and carefully closed them in my Nepali primer. They were starting to paper the trail. I was walking on blessings. Around me the Himalayan cedar and dwarf banyans were embellished with this magnificent lit-ter. I broke into a jog, wanting to make the peak before the ritual ended. The old man was coming down the trail. The humpbacked ruin of a giant, he gripped unvarnished hard-wood canes in either hand, deploying them with great dexterity and spryness. Along with the shuffling of his thin legs, his quick four-legged gait made me think of one of those insects, water-striders, skittering over a pond. He was simply dressed—straw hat, grey slacks, a white shirt, the sleeves rolled up his scarecrow arms. He carried no pack. A muddy prayer tissue affixed to the bottom of a shoe flashed white as he moved. The deep bunker of bone housing his eyes lent a fleeting impression of severity, yet the eyes, I saw now, had a burnt-out serenity, as in the aftermath of a long illness or other purging. Anyway, I was eager to reach the peak, so I failed to stop and talk to him, to ask if he had made it up there and how it had been. I gave him the Nepali greeting, *Namaste*—literally, "I salute the godhood within you"—and hurried on.